the Truth About Diamonds

Is Stranger Than Fiction

In her electrifying first novel, Nicole Richie tells the sensational story of Chloe Parker, a rock royalty princess and a card-carrying member of Hollywood's inner circle. At the age of seven, Chloe was adopted by a music superstar and his wife, transforming her life from rags to riches. What followed was a wild childhood distinguished by parties with movie stars and rock idols, run-ins with the press and the police, and a subsequent stint in rehab.

Suddenly Chloe shoots to instant fame as a spokesmodel for a national advertising campaign. When her long-lost birth father appears out of nowhere and her best friend betrays her, she must struggle to keep it all together—her sobriety, her friendships, and her integrity—despite the betrayals of those around her. Ultimately, Chloe comes spectacularly into her own, achieving stardom in her own right and finding true love.

the Truth
Diamo

A NOVEL ★ A NOVEL ★ A NOVEL ★ A NOVEL ★ A NOVEL

NIC

About
nds

A NOVEL ★ A NOVEL ★ A NOVEL ★ A NOVEL ★ A NOVEL

OLE RICHIE

REGAN

An Imprint of HarperCollinsPublishers

A hardcover edition of this book was published in 2005 by Regan, an imprint of HarperCollins Publishers.

FIRST PAPERBACK EDITION PUBLISHED IN 2006

Designed by Judy Abbate

The Library of Congress has cataloged the hardcover edition as follows:

Richie, Nicole.
    The truth about diamonds : a novel / Nicole Richie.—1st ed.
    x,226 p.:ill.; 24 cm.
    ISBN 10: 0-06-082048-9
    ISBN 13: 978-0-06-082048-0
        1. Celebrities—California—Los Angeles—Fiction. 2. Hollywood (Los Angeles, Calif.)—Fiction.

                                      2006276160

ISBN 13: 978-0-06-113733-4 (pbk.)
ISBN 10: 0-06-113733-2 (pbk.)

06 07 08 09 10 WBC/RRD 10 9 8 7 6 5 4 3 2 1

To Miles and Sofia . . .
the two most precious diamonds.

Diamond in the Rough

I KNOW SOME PEOPLE out there are thinking, *Why is this girl writing a book? Sure, she has style, has survived tabloid rumors, looks cute in her various mug shots, and has a hit TV show . . . but what has she actually done to deserve a book?*

These are the same things I said to myself when I was approached to do one of those tell-alls that my friends and I used to speed-read on the beach in Malibu when we couldn't get our hands on the latest *Vogue*.

I'll tell you what I told the editor: Writing an autobiography will be a lot more problematic than you think—it may be a simple life on reality TV, but in reality *reality*, life is anything but simple. Also, I'm only twenty-four, and, although I have famous parents, have lived the glamorous life, got arrested (three times!), finished rehab before I finished my teens, starred on a hit show, have started recording a CD, and am now sporting a ring given to me by a totally hot fiancé, I haven't lived even *half* of my life yet.

Just in case you did buy *The Truth About Diamonds* seeking an autobiography, here it is in a nutshell: I'm too ADD to keep up with the latest Hollywood gossip; making me *the* friend to spill your secrets to. Tabloid rumors would only bother me if I thought for a second that people take tabloids seriously. My favorite foods are sushi, pizza, and Mr. Chow's, in that order. My favorite movies are *The Wizard of Oz, Breakfast at Tiffany's, Welcome to the Dollhouse*, and *The NeverEnding Story*, but I gravitate toward guilty pleasures like *Center Stage*. My heroine is Drew Barrymore, whom I admire for achieving all she has after going through so much. I believe in astrology and magic. I get pissed off when people tickle me.

And I don't have any secrets left to tell.

One thing I've learned since detoxing from drugs and from self-doubt is how much I treasure my family and the real friends who've been with me through all my ups and downs—they're more valuable than the Costume National African-print dress that gets you the "Look of the Week" in *People*.

There are only a few people left in my life whom I trust implicitly and who totally trust me back. I used to think that was bad, but then I realized the truth: True friends are like diamonds—bright, beautiful, valuable, and *always* in style. You only need a few diamonds—including one for the finger.

My one-for-the-finger is the guy of every girl's dreams. Okay, so I still have a crush on Jeff Goldblum (don't ask; there's just something about him), but my fiancé keeps Jeff off my mind.

Another diamond in my life? Meet Chloe Parker, the star of this novel. Having fun was Chloe's original (and least destructive) drug. Unfortunately, she wound up trying all the bad ones, too—more on that later.

How did Chloe come into my life? We were both adopted by famous men in the music industry—her adopted dad was a superstar music producer in the 1970s who became president of a major record label in the 1980s, back when a job like that was still a big deal—so we spent a lot of years bonding in recording studios on ratty couches in the middle of the night, meeting Madonna, dancing for Ray Charles and being so pissed off when he didn't look, and owning the first BlackBerrys ever invented.

We were known for the one-two punch of our themed birthday parties since we were born in the same month, and are the ultimate Virgos. The year that Lionel and Brenda threw me a *Batman* birthday party at which my entire backyard was transformed into Gotham City and my room into the Batcave, Chloe's parents had a *Little Mermaid* party with *real dolphins*. We weren't even doing this ironically at the time—we thought this stuff was normal.

Later, if I didn't feel like dealing with the paparazzi, she could even pass for me—all I had to do was give Chloe my oversized, vintage Dior sunglasses and my Stella McCartney jacket, and they'd chase her instead. But those days are over. Even though Chloe witnessed all the drama I've been exposed to since my life virtually became a live feed, she's currently experiencing firsthand how fame is like a giant magnifying glass—and that only a perfect diamond looks good *that* close up.

Is anyone perfect? No. All the people in this novel are fictional, but like real people, they're flawed. And even though I adore her and she's one of the greatest girls I know, my diamond in the rough, Chloe, is no exception.

PART One

Before

CHAPTER 1

Reserved Seating

CHLOE PARKER would be a terrible role model if she were famous. Trouble is that she was about to be.

It started innocently enough, or as innocent as you can get on the dance floor of one of the hottest clubs in L.A.

The nightclubs of L.A. are like soap operas, except they're not *Days of Our Lives*; they're more like *Passions*—crazy stuff happens, and no one bats a fake eyelash. There's always some bizarre drama that plays out every night, and everyone in the cast—I mean, *everyone*—is great looking, stoned, and/or drunk. It's like a traveling freak show that stars the youngest and hottest in Hollywood. It's about fun, and sex, and pseudo-danger.

Chloe Parker was practically born in a club. It's like she spontaneously generated one night in 1981 during a fourteen-minute remix. As a child, she could dance before she could walk and sing before she could talk. Dressed in a tie-dyed onesie and a tutu, her head a tangle of golden curls, Chloe was destined to haunt the clubs of her adoptive city as soon as humanly possible.

Chloe had been going to the hottest clubs in Hollywood since she was this many, wearing L.A. Gear sneakers everywhere she went. Like me, Chloe has always been tiny, which meant we could both sneak into The Viper Room under the noses of the bouncers when we were thirteen. She was a kid partying with adults who treated her like a peer. Every important marker of her life had to do with clubbing. She wore her first bra to a club. She went out *without* a bra for the first time to a club. Her first kiss, her first crush on a gay guy, the first time she saw Jimmy Choo sandals, the first time someone passed her a joint— all happened in a club.

As a kid, Chloe would stand behind the DJ booth and dance, and the DJ could tell if he had the vibe right just by monitoring her movements. Like Holly Golightly in Madonna-wannabe rags, Chloe had the ability to not only be *in* the moment, but to *create* it.

It helped that she always gave herself little jobs to do to make everyone happier. She'd hand out Dixie cups of water if people were looking overheated, or she would fan them with the sleeve of one of the 12-inch records the DJ was playing. She was the Disco Granny reincarnated.

In those days, Chloe was like that—so pure, all heart and soul. To see her smile would have the same effect on a roomful of sweaty strangers as the DJ playing a classic, crowd-pleasing track. She could be like a little sliver of the sun—her glow lit them up.

Chloe's mailing address might have been her mom Peggy's place in Bel Air, but the place to find her—and more importantly the place where she was finding herself—was whatever party was hottest at the moment.

That night, it was Mode, a converted church on Cahuenga just north of Hollywood. Unfortunately, all of us were discovering a new side to Chloe—a scary one.

Chloe didn't need drugs to have fun. I mean, drugs would be double-bad for an addictive personality like hers, and I think she knew it. But she was drawn to them for the same reasons any young person may be—drugs seemed glam, and exciting, and reckless. Being high was intriguing; it made her feel alive. Drugs were everywhere in every club. And drugs took the place of love.

But along with whatever her other drugs du jour were, Chloe was as addicted to the club scene as she was a part of it.

To get to our booth, Chloe aggressively stomped up the staircase of Mode, a multi-tiered architectural maze with flashing lights and music so loud it felt like it invaded you, like a virus. Just as everyone in L.A. had to climb the social ladder, Chloe and all the rest of us had to climb three flights of stairs to get to the VIP level at Mode. Sometimes, scaling the social ladder was easier and faster than making it up those stairs, which were usually choked with hangers-on, wasted fans, and undercover tabloid reporters. Chloe wasn't nationally famous yet, but she was a glittering part of the youth party scene, and reporters were smart enough to know that where there's smoke, there's fire.

On her way up the stairs, Chloe started to pass two Asian girls, one tall and the other short and squat, who were bobbing their heads to the end of Kanye West's *Gold-digger*. They both wore hip-huggers and expensive-looking belly shirts. They were not holding drinks, and their pupils were not dilated. Even in her chemically altered state, Chloe pegged them immediately: They were definitely magazine reporters.

At Mode, people acted up, hooked up, and threw up, and the paparazzi stood outside to shoot the stars as they went in looking fabulous and staggered out totally gone. Guess which kinds of photos got published? You're right! *Both* kinds got published. From what I heard, an exclusive shot of a new couple could earn up to fifty grand from a celebrity weekly. The price would triple if the photogs could shoot inside, but the iron-clad rule was *no* cameras and *no* reporters in the clubs. That was part of what stoked the glamour and mystery. No one really knew what went on inside. The doormen played, too. They were judge and jury when it came to letting people in and keeping people out. That meant the warm-up act for the freak show usually started outside.

Guys with money? Yup. But the doormen tried to keep

the ratio of guys to girls at about ten to one. They wanted all the Brad Pitt wannabes to open their wallets while competing for the handful of Angelinas.

Ordinary people? Nope. "This ain't Wal-Mart!" They were stuck just waiting in a line that never moved, praying that they'll be let in to party with the stars. By ordinary, I mean nonfamous, which includes big-talking producers and cheesy hustlers droning on about connections and waving cash and business cards at the hard-bodied TV stars who may take them to the next level on the business side—or who may just put out in a moment of poor judgment. That was the fantasy: with the right look and a little luck and pluck, their lives could change— not just overnight but in the span of a three-minute song with a bass that felt like adrenaline coursing through their veins.

Sexy girls like Chloe Parker *always* got in.

It turned out that the reporterettes worked in tandem and had their routine down pat for when Chloe came within striking distance. One casually blocked Chloe's path with a gentle nudge, while the other made contact.

"Hey, you're Chloe, aren't you?" the chubby girl asked, her voice trembling. "Chloe—"

"Parker. Yes!" Chloe smiled at the girl and her skinny-me, who had touched Chloe's bare shoulder lightly and apologized for "accidentally" bumping into her.

"I see you around all the time," she continued, shouting into Chloe's ear to be heard above the intro to Gwen

Stefani's "Hollaback Girl." "You look great tonight. You *always* look great. Cute outfit!"

"Thanks!" Chloe knew she was radiant in a yellow Missoni classic print minidress and her trademark magnificent diamond chandelier earrings. They were real diamonds, a gift from her father when she turned sixteen, and every girl in L.A. had coveted them ever since.

"Missoni is *so* the label right now," the girl continued, boldly feeling up the fabric of Chloe's dress.

The spiel was always the same. If you've talked with one undercover reporter, you've talked with them all. Reporter starts with small talk. Prey loosens. Reporter seeks trusting relationship. Prey loosens more. But knowing the convo was going to be three minutes tops, the reporter can never hold back long before moving in for the kill. It always felt like a giant clock was ticking right over your shoulder.

"Hey, I'm so sorry to bug you," the reporter lied, "but I'm Liz Chan with *Bitz Weekly*." She said it quickly, like she was yanking a Band-Aid. *Bitz* was one of the less vicious tabs, but all of us had been on their fashion pages for better or for worse. "I'm one of the nightlife reporters, and I know I'm not supposed to bug you or talk to you inside—it's kind of an unspoken agreement we have with the manager—but I just have to ask or my editor's going to kill me, and I'll get fired and lose my apartment, and yada, yada, yada down life's highway to hell, but—"

"What's the question?" Chloe asked cheerfully. "My

favorite color is gold, I don't have a dog, and I think Johnny Depp is the hottest guy of all time. Oh, and no comment on TomKat. Is that enough? Did one of them answer your question?" She was already jonesing for a Cosmotini to take the edge off the oxycontin.

"No," the reporter said, either grinning or grimacing. You can't tell one from the other in the darkness of a club, which always either helps a lot or leads to huge mistakes. "I wanted to know if you knew whether or not Nicole is really doing *The Simple Life 4* . . . ?"

Chloe's mood soured. She'd never begrudged me any of my success—she was always my biggest cheerleader—but she was definitely getting tired of being someone connected to the topic of conversation instead of *being* the topic herself. Chloe didn't have a TV show like mine—she was just one of those locally legendary Hollywood kids—rich but not famous, stylish but not on the cover of *In-Style*. She was never jealous of me, but she'd always wanted to do something on TV herself. It's hard *not* to aspire to fame when your own parents are famous. It's like taking over the family business.

Chloe smiled away the unintended insult.

"Ask Nicole," Chloe said pleasantly enough. It was very "let them eat cake" since there was no way this chick was getting within fifty feet of our VIP booth.

Like a snake on water, Chloe slithered past the reporters and up the last set of stairs to the exclusive third tier toward me, our friends, and our protective booth, where no reporters had ever dared to show their faces. Chloe flashed her smile like an I.D. at the bouncer controlling access to that level, and she was in. Getting into Mode—the hottest club in town that month—and getting up to the VIP level was like being told you were good enough to go on living.

Everyone was there that night, the whole clique we'd acquired somewhere between birth and our early twenties: Joey, Carrie, Mikela, Lanford, and *moi*. We were crammed into the most prized booth like a gaggle of kids on a monstrous Tilt-a-Whirl, smoking, drinking, drugging, and/or gossiping in our best effort to recapture the magic we'd seen in archival photos from Studio 54's heyday. We were nothing if not unoriginal.

The RESERVED plaque in the middle of our table next to the ice buckets always had "Rock Royalty" written on it—a joke from Sid, our friend who ran the club. All of us had connections to the recording industry, which was the glue that held us together.

Joseph Able came from hot stock. His mom was a sexy has-been movie star, and his dad was a country singer with two gold records for every year he'd been alive. Their marriage was over before the pregnancy was, which suited Joey fine since he always said toys were a by-product of parental (and in his dad's case, *prenatal*) guilt. Joey had gorgeous, chestnut-brown hair that he wore long, ironically in the same cut his father had worked decades earlier. Joey's best feature was his skin, something girls always notice in guys and guys never notice in themselves. He had a complexion that was smoother and softer than the linen at the Four Seasons. He was also a major talent behind a piano and wrote songs that literally squeezed your heart till the tears streamed from your eyes. Oh, and Joey was a messed up junkie.

Chloe had dated Joey a few months back when both of them were in self-deluded periods of sobriety. Joey had tried to kick his three-year heroin habit by studying some kind of transcendentalist Zen thing. That had pretty much just turned him into a transcendentalist Zen junkie. They ended badly when word got out that he was still on drugs and was cheating on Chloe. Since then, they'd acted like the whole thing never happened. Chloe couldn't bear to stop being friends with Joey, a guy she'd always crushed on so heavily. I always suspected he was the one who really got Chloe going on heroin, and it made me sick to picture them doing that nasty brown stuff together. One thing was for sure: His complexion's days were numbered. Joey was trouble, but I loved him to death—I was just hoping I wouldn't have to.

Next to Joey the Junkie sat Carrie the Queen, raven-haired daughter of authentic rock royalty (her daddy was knighted, she liked to remind me, while mine was a prince of pop "in name only"), and her mom was the world's second supermodel. She was chatting with a cute guy who was leaning over the table to make sure the rest of the room saw a little ass cleavage. I thought he might be her new boyfriend, but then I saw him jotting notes as she feverishly spoke into his ear telling him things to say in front of the reporters, and I realized he was just her new assistant. If you knew how Carrie Markee spent her days, you'd laugh so hard at the idea of her having an assistant. A big day for Carrie was getting a mani-pedi. Mainly, all she did was shop, work out, and go to her colorist so often no one even remembered her real hair color. You couldn't even guess from the eyebrows because they were penciled on. I know because one night when she was passed out, I rubbed one off with my finger. No lie.

Why did Carrie *need* an assistant? From what I could tell, all the guy did was alert her when she got a page on her BlackBerry, and that wasn't often. Carrie Markee was proving to the world that you *could* be both unpopular and part of the in crowd. She's the kind of girl who'd get pregnant just to have an abortion to brag about.

At the other end of the booth was Mikela, a J.Lo-built flower-grandchild brunette infamous for posing for a nudie website literally *on* her eighteenth birthday. The site had a countdown going for two years leading up to the magic moment, and the resulting Mikela pages had resulted in enough downloads to make her an international sex goddess even before she got her high school diploma. She was raised in a Malibu mansion built on the feel-good pop songs her dad had written—he had a gift for thinking up clever things to rhyme with "love," like "above" and "think of."

Why was Mikela so needy when she'd never wanted anything in life that she couldn't or didn't have? Because the one thing that *all* of us wanted, the thing her dad's songs were always about, was the one thing she actually didn't have. Trouble was, none of us knew where to find it—not then anyway.

I guess we were less like friends and more like a dysfunctional support group, bonded in equal parts romantic misery and social momentum.

Rounding out the group and wedged in the booth right next to me that night was Lanford Watts—tall, blond, boyishly handsome, and uncharacteristically sweet for a billionaire, his dad had made his fortune in plastic. Not exactly music-related, you might be thinking, but his dad's company made everything from the records the club's DJ Ray was spinning to the vinyl that barely covered Christina Aguilera to the guitar straps on the Fenders so many of our parents played for a living. As Lanny liked to say, "There would be no rock without plastic."

I always thought Lanny was nice to a San Andreas fault. Growing up, he was the only one of us who actually had any kind of a job. When he was eight, he'd hawk newspapers. On Sunday mornings, his father would buy a stack of the *L.A. Times* on the way to brunch at Nate 'n' Al's, the ultimate Beverly Hills diner. He'd have little Lanford stand outside the door and sell, sell, sell. It wasn't that he got rich this way. In fact, buying papers retail to resell them for the same price had wound up teaching Lanny that it's not always about the money; it's about keeping busy. He also ended up knowing absolutely *everyone* in Beverly Hills, from old-timers like Doris Day to A-listers like Mike Meyers and even Chelsea Clinton, who he dated for nine days without the media ever knowing.

As soon as Chloe cleared the stairs, she waved at us and hit the DJ booth to hug DJ Ray, a candidate for the nicest guy ever. Nothing had ever happened between them, but they were longtime friends. They had bonded one night five years earlier at an edgy club in WeHo when the line for the bathroom was so long that a wasted Chloe had wandered into his DJ booth and peed all over his feet. It was unfortunate, but DJ Ray was forgiving, and Chloe was someone who collected forgiveness in the same way we'd once tried collecting everything with Strawberry Shortcake's picture on it. I'd always thought there was a connection there. Ray made the music, and Chloe danced to it.

I was drinking some fancy imported water out of a supersexy bottle. From where I was seated, I could tell that Chloe had been drinking something out of a bottle earlier, too, but it had been a lot stronger than water judging by her unsteady walk. Alcohol was going to be just one of several problems for her that night.

Another problem that would soon haunt Chloe was her equally intoxicating and addictive boyfriend, Chip Zou, a bass player in an eye-rolling rap-rock band that played all the clubs but still hadn't been signed. Okay, he wasn't really a boyfriend—at least not in my book. Poser? Hanger-on? Yes and yes. Boyfriend? Hardly. I think it was obvious to everyone that Chip just wanted anything Chloe could rub off on him. If he got a little sex out of her, even better. He never said it, but girls know this stuff.

Guys are so transparent most of the time. Unless, of course, they're dating you, in which case they are utter mysteries.

Anyway, Chip had bad skin, bad manners, and a bad haircut. Some of us in our group had our own personal fragrance. Chip just stank. He smelled like onions and stale clove cigs with a hint of those crappy body sprays salesgirls force on guys in malls. Oh, I'm being a big bitch, but there really were *so* many reasons not to like him, at least one for every reason Chloe had for being blindly, madly head-over-heels for him.

If I hated him this much already, how much do you think I was going to like him once we'd actually been introduced?

Chloe abandoned Ray abruptly when she spotted Chip, running over to him and throwing her arms around him, kissing him like she was eating dinner. Maybe some E was mixed in? As unmoved as Chip was, Ray looked semi-crushed, like someone had just scratched his favorite record.

"Oh God," Mikela said to us, hoisting her Stella Mc-Cartney onto her oft-downloaded shoulder. "Chloe's new one is *such* a rebound."

"Totally," Carrie agreed, always a parrot. "She'll *never* get past what Ana did to her."

Joey *was* the dude she was allegedly rebounding from; he *was* what Ana had done to Chloe, so he was guiltily silent.

It was kind of bad form to gossip about one of our own, but I knew the girls were right. Sometimes it seemed like Chloe had hooked up with every bad-news boy on the map—including Joey.

As if on cue, Chloe took Chip by the paw and brought him over to our booth—wow, this was a serious relationship. Chloe was going to introduce him to her family at long last.

"Here we go," Lanny said under his breath, leaning into me to brace himself.

"Everyone, everyone," Chloe said, gesturing awkwardly at Chip, who after that kiss was now wearing more lipstick than Chloe was. "This is my *boyfriend*, Chip Zou. I want you guys to be really nice to him and like him a lot, okay?" She laughed, and Chip barely nodded at us. All of us smiled and kept our mouths shut.

In Hollywood, you rarely have to introduce people formally by name—everybody *knows* who everybody else is. It's more a matter of just presenting newcomers, like, "Okay, here is a fresh victim."

I'm not judgmental, but I can judge mentals. Chip was at best a random and at worst a major druggie. As far as I could tell, he wasn't going to be worth the Crisco he seemed to use as styling gel. Our own group had enough problems without inviting in people with the same problems and absolutely no self-awareness about them.

Without a word being said, Chip just kind of slouched away from us, pretending to see a friend across the room. He started hovering around Jesse Metcalfe, acting like they knew each other. It was like an episode of *Desperate Clubkids.*

"Hey, Chip, nice to meet you, too!" Joey said, sarcastically clapping his hands like a child being handed cotton candy for the first time.

"Did I ever do him?" Mikela wondered aloud.

Thankfully, Chloe's hearing was anything but bionic.

Ignoring the icy reception we'd given her newest new guy, Chloe plopped into the last available spot on the ultra-suede seat, right next to me. I could see she was sweating like Whitney Houston and talking, talking, talking too much with her hands. She wouldn't stay seated, either, getting up to make every point like she couldn't restrain her own energy. I asked her a bazillion times to sit her ass down, but she just twitched like a robot about to short-circuit, finally trotting over to the bar.

Take it from a recovered addict—she was on several things at once, but mainly she was sky high on coke.

It's not like most of us hadn't been in that very same place at some point over the years—some of us were actually *still* in a similar, if not quite as dangerous, place, I thought as I eyed Joey—but Chloe had been the last of us to get sucked into the drug void.

"Are you worried about Chloe?" I asked Lanny, who seemed to be watching her as intently as I was.

"In what way?" he asked cautiously, always discreet. "She's Chloe. I mean, look at this group. She's not the first person I usually have to worry about."

"I know," I said, "but she's way high and out of control. She's acting like a balloon some kid let go of. She's not . . ." I struggled for the right words ". . . like she used to be. You know? She's not Chloe."

"First of all, Chloe's not normal in any way," Lanny said. "No one here is, or we wouldn't exactly be here."

"But it's like every time I see her now, she's totally wasted. You only see her in clubs lately, where it's to be expected. But I'm talking about *all the time*. That's never been her M.O. I mean, not when she was all . . . *happy*."

He nodded toward Joey, who was swigging a vodka and cranberry.

"Yeah, him, too," I said. "But look at Chloe—"

"Three-quarters of the guys here are looking at her and quite a few chicks, too. They don't seem to notice anything wrong."

I ignored him. "She's ready to combust. I don't know, Lanny. I just . . . sense it. It's like she's going to blow."

"She will if Chip gets his way."

"Wise-ass, that's my friend!"

"Mine, too," Lanny said, giving in to me. "Hey, Chloe!"

he called out. "Chloe! Over here, girl!" She had drifted away from the bar, and Lanny's voice got lost in the music. Then she just took off down the stairs as if she was falling standing up. By the time either of us could have torn ourselves out of the VIP booth, it would've already been too late.

Chloe Spaces

W HOA!" LANNY SAID, like two seconds later. He was pointing downstairs, over the balcony. I followed his finger and spotted Chloe. That's when I knew why she'd made her dash—Ana Cannon, the pudgy Puerto Rican princess with her own Telemundo reality show had just walked in. Ana had a way of entering a room with all the subtlety of a sexual assault.

Like all of us, Ana had been born into good fortune. Her dad, Carlito, was a hippie rocker who'd fried his brains out decades ago, but his sixth wife, Goldie, knew how to milk his iconic status, turning his dementia into dinero. Together, man-and-wife were a certified nightmare, which apparently was a dominant gene. Unfortunately, musical talent—in Ana's case—seemed to have skipped a generation. She did, however, inherit her mother's acid tongue and her dad's taste for acid, among other controlled substances.

That night, Ana walked into Mode wearing a dress almost identical to Chloe's—only pink. I happened to know that Chloe's dress was sold to her as a one-of-a-kind, the type of statement garment that's not about wearing it better, but about wearing it. And yet there was Ana, three times Chloe's size, wearing an amazingly similar dress that was three times as colorful. Now all the shots Chloe had posed for outside would only be published, if at all, to make fun of her for copying the far more famous Ana.

"Oh, my Versace . . ." I muttered to Lanny as we watched things go from bad to worse.

As Mikela and Carrie had already psychically brought up, Ana had done something unspeakable to Chloe: She had started regularly messing around with Joey while he and Clo were still an item. When Chloe learned that her man was double-dipping with the likes of Ana (and that he liked dressing up in Ana's panties, according to a blind item on Stawker.com—the one part of the story Joey convincingly denied), she'd been devastated, embarrassed, and grossed out. It was hard for any of us to picture deadsexy Joey with fugly Ana. Joey, for his part, always just pointed to Ana and said, "This is your dick on drugs."

"Guys, guys," Lanny said, "maybe this won't be as bad as we think . . . ?"

"I'm sure she's over it," Joey said, clearly irritated that circumstances were shining a bright light on his Jude Law moment with Ana yet again.

"Yeah," Mikela agreed, "I was at Tracey Ross last week with Chloe, and Ana was there—they were, like, face-to-face. Chloe was totally chill."

Chloe had managed to keep her rage under wraps, but now they were in a *club*. There was a totally different etiquette here than at any *boutique*. For one thing, the staff of a club will have you back no matter what you do. The staff of a boutique will ban you like last season's flop accessory if you disrupt their precious ambience, reminding the clientele that money can't buy serenity.

Unfortunately, our group's optimism was misplaced. Maybe it was the pounding music, the garish dresses, or the sprint down the stairs. It might've been the coke. But whatever it was, it was *on*.

Chloe exchanged words with a shiny, shellacked Ana, whose outlook on makeup application fit somewhere between the circus and the morgue. It went from conversation to confrontation pretty fast, with Chloe holding a champagne flute like it was a lightsaber.

"I'm not *asking* you!" I heard Chloe shout. It was loud enough to carry across the club *over* the thumping soundtrack. I could barely hear Lanny right next to me, but Chloe I could hear fine. "I am *telling* you! You started screwing him way before we broke up, and everybody knows it!" Well, they did now.

Chloe drained her drink down her throat in the beat between ending her sentence and the beginning of Ana's reply.

"I don't know what you're *talking about*, Clo—you are,

like, one of my *very best friends*!" Ana protested, wide-eyed. She couldn't sing. She couldn't act either, apparently. "I'd never, ever do anything like that to you!"

"You denying it only makes it worse!" Chloe raged, slamming her empty glass on the nearest table. Was it my imagination, or was DJ Ray lowering the volume a bit so everyone could hear? I looked over at him and saw him staring at Chloe with an intensity that seemed more than just ambulance chasing. Hmmm.

Ana seemed a bit rattled by Chloe's venom. "What's your problem, anyway?" She fixed an exhausted strap on her beefy shoulder. "I thought you had a new boyfriend anyway."

Chip happened to be showing some eager club chica his latest tattoo, tiny script on his right index finger that read Carpay Diem [sic].

"That's not the point!" Now Chloe was really pissed and out of control in a way I'd never seen her. From where I was, it looked like her eyes were rolling back in a combination of disgust and drunken stupor. "The point is you did something so, so terrible to me, and you are not even decent enough to admit it! Even Joey admits it, and he's got a reason to be embarrassed about it!" She was subconsciously picking up Ana's thick Puerto Rican accent—all of us seemed to do it when we talked with her. Good to know the phenomenon also happened when yelling and screaming.

"Chloe, I don't know who you are talking to," Ana insisted, "but they're *not* your real friends because they're *lying*!"

Then, like, out of *nowhere*, Ana just started laughing—softly at first and then a lot harder, a huge, sloppy belly laugh as ladylike as a belch or a mustache. It was this shrill, car-alarm guffaw that could just as easily be taken to mean, "You're right, but I'll never admit it!" or "This accusation is so silly, I can only laugh about it!" Everyone was openly watching, even DJ Ray, whose distraction from his job showed with a pretty effed up transition from some feel-good trance to a tweaked-out version of *You Give Love a Bad Name*. I don't know if he did it in Chloe's honor, but I wouldn't have been surprised—a good DJ doesn't spin in a vacuum, and DJ Ray had a sixth sense about things. More than a lot of us, I think he had a special appreciation for the obvious identity crisis Chloe was going through.

Ray used to be fat. He was 5 feet 11 inches by the end of high school, but he weighed close to 300 pounds. It was like his growth spurt had happened horizontally. Aiding his body's rebellion was his appetite for downing Big Macs, Whoppers, and Double Doubles with the same enthusiasm he DJed his emotions with pot, pills, and anything else handy to numb the pain. He'd successfully rehabbed at the same time I did—we'd hung out while saying good-bye to being strung-out—and a gastric bypass made him half the man he used to be. Still, everyone but Ray knew there was a totally cool dude hanging out in there somewhere. Chloe, I think, saw this clearest of all—when she wasn't whacked out and preparing to kick Ana's ass back to Puerto Rico.

At that moment, Chloe couldn't notice anything other than Ana's manic laugh. Ana kept bending over and grabbing her stomach. I guess the laugh was her attempt at pretending this whole stole-your-boyfriend incident was a big joke, something they could laugh off. Maybe Ana thought she'd disarm Chloe with it or at least dull the edge. It so didn't work.

Chloe snapped. "Bitch!" she howled like a scene out of *The Grudge*.

Belatedly, I tried to push my way out of my booth and down the stairs. The trouble was that everyone was frozen solid in place, like they were watching a car careening over a bridge in slow-mo. Chloe must've been taking Pilates on the sly because even wasted she managed to stay balanced while landing a kick right on Ana's already pretty undesirable nose. And she did this in Manolos—really cute ones, too, which is weird because I hadn't noticed them until the left one was covering Ana's face.

Ana toppled back onto someone's table (their faces read: "Stories forever!"), her legs sky high revealing a pair of granny panties about as cool as something you'd find abandoned in a Fresno Laundromat, and I finally squeezed my way free. But before Ana could regroup and before I could get down to the first floor, Chloe had woven through the crowd and bolted out the door into a sea of flashes.

The two undercover reporters, drunk on drama, each thrust micro cassette recorders into my face. "Any comment?" they asked in unison.

"Holy shit," Lanny said, catching up to me. "What was *that* about?"

"Good-bye, Chloe," I mumbled, shaking my head. "Hello, *Bitz Weekly*."

Joey came down next, then Carrie, who descended the stairs like she was making a grand entrance, even though all the excitement was clearly over.

"Should I have my *assistant* go after her?" she asked everyone and no one, emphasizing the word assistant. "Because I will totally do it."

The last thing I heard before we left was the chubby Asian reporter asking Joey in a voice tinged with equal parts terror and titillation, "Dude, tell me you didn't *seriously* wear those panties . . . ?"

CHAPTER 3

The Club Baby Vanishes

BY THE TIME we hit the pavement outside Mode, several things had happened: Lanny had given his cell phone number to the *Bitzches* and promised them an exclusive story about the time he dated Chelsea Clinton in exchange for them not following us. Chip had abandoned his new admirer and taken off after Chloe, beating us to the punch. And Chloe had disappeared into the warm summer night.

We split up to look for her, severely testing the paparazzi's organizational skills since they had to immediately decide which of us to tail. Thank God Britney Spears (and, oh yeah, Kevin Federline) showed up, oblivious to what was going on. In the confusion, the cameras gravitated to her, and I was able to sneak in the direction of Chloe's car, the same way I'd seen Chip going.

Even though I knew it was useless, I text Chloe: "where r u I want 2 come get u."

A second later, I received a message from Sid: "Ana so pissed at clo!!!" He was probably enjoying this—Mode was for sure getting press when the tabloids came out on Wednesday.

Mikela was right behind Sid with the text: "where u going next?"

Thanks for caring, Mikela. Chloe's life could be in danger, and Mikela just wanted to avoid going to a dead nightclub later on.

I headed down Cahuenga to the place where all of us were parked and saw Chloe's tiny silver Merc. No Chloe, but at least she wasn't driving under the influence of, um, *everything*. Finally, I heard her.

"Give it to me! It's mine!" she was shouting. "I paid for it!"

Chloe was in a lot yelling at Chip, who was greedily sniffing the crotch between his thumb and finger. Coke. You do it and think it totally sets you free. Then you find out you're way worse off than you were to begin with and thousands of dollars poorer. I mean, just look at Chip. Or just *smell* him. He was a walking scratch-and-sniff "Just Say No" billboard.

Next to them was Chip's ride, one of those hybrids like Leo drives. Some guy that I'd never seen was in the driver's seat, smoking a cig and ignoring the drama. He was counting a wad of cash that I was guessing probably came from Chloe's daddy's bank account.

"Why should I?" Chip yelled back at Chloe. "After what you did? You just completely embarrassed us!"

"What *I* just did?" Chloe railed. "What about you and that girl? You were *all over her*! And now you're stealing my shit!"

I stopped walking for a second and watched them. I thought back to when Chloe was a little girl, a total innocent. I thought about her in school, always in trouble and yet always able to come through it unscathed, sometimes for reasons no one, including I, could fathom. How could someone who had led such a blessed life end up like this? Why was she tussling with Chip when there were so many other guys who'd die to be with her?

"C'mon," Chloe drug-whined to Chip, "give it!"

She grabbed Chip's shoulder and spun him around while he was in the middle of another sniff, and the vial that held the coke fell with a delicate clink. Such a pretty sound and then a tiny patch of the asphalt was covered in snow. It was unrecoverable unless either of them planned to make like an anteater and snort the ground. That's when the dude totally lost it.

Chip turned and clocked Chloe on the left side of her face. It sounded awful—I'll never forget the pop. At the time, I thought he'd smashed her face in. She tumbled to the ground just as fast as any girl ever hit by any guy—you fall just as fast and just as hard whether you're smacked in Hollywood, Cleveland, Brooklyn, or Guadala-freaking-jara. When Chloe was done falling, she was sitting on her ass in a funky puddle, the perfect metaphor for the pond of loser juice she'd been swimming upstream in ever since drugs had won her over.

"Chloe!" I yelled, hurrying toward them. I'd been working out, but even though I looked down on Chip in many ways, he definitely could have snapped me in two. I just didn't care. In that moment, I knew I had to get to Chloe.

The guy in the driver's seat got out quickly and helped Chip pull Chloe off the ground, probably more to cover up what had just happened than out of any concern for her well-being. She didn't seem to be putting up any kind of fight. She was stunned, stoned, or both.

By the time I got within ten feet of them, Chloe was already in the passenger seat, a disheveled wreck. Her MAC makeup—she always only wore eyeliner, no base, and an unblended shade of lipstick to match her outfit—was no match for her despondent tears.

She turned her head and saw me. Her face, streaked with eyeliner, was starting to match the oil-splotched parking lot. But her eyes were what scared me. They were blank and terrified, like she'd lost touch with reality. The guy I didn't know was at the wheel in a heartbeat and turning the key in the ignition. He revved the engine loudly as I shouted, "Chloe! These guys are jerks! Don't go with them! Get out!"

She didn't make a move, and the doors were still open, so I reached in and tried to get her seatbelt undone to pull her out. All of them looked at me like I was the crazy one.

"C'mon, Clo," I said as calmly as I could. "You *have* to get out of this car."

She reached out to me, but her hand was a limp noodle. Then her so-called boyfriend started yelling from the backseat, "Go! Go! Go!"

The guy shifted into drive and floored it with no warning. The speedy take-off slammed the doors shut, and I pulled away just in time to avoid a dragging incident that I think might have provided pinkisthenewblog.com with fodder for a week. Oh, yes—the paparazzi were clicking away and had been the whole time. I guess the Federlines had gone inside the club quickly, leaving them free to pursue Plan B.

The hybrid from hell hung a right and headed north to the Hills. I thought I heard Chloe crying, but I'm sure I just imagined it. Carrie, Joey, and Lanny came running up, all three uncharacteristically speechless.

Then I looked down and saw it, one of those amazing, diamond chandelier earrings Chloe had been wearing. It sparkled against the charcoal asphalt and even more brilliantly against the inky black night sky when I held it up to the street lights. I knew it must have worked itself out of Chloe's ear when Chip smacked her. Reverently, I tucked it into my clutch.

The night was sweltering, the smell of pizza was coming from somewhere, and cars were tooling past in a haze of exhaust and laughter. The young people of Los Angeles had places to be, and they weren't about to stop at the sight of some kids standing around wondering if their friend was going to be okay.

Welcome to Hollywood. Ain't it glam?

CHAPTER 4

Dream Girls

THAT NIGHT, I had the weirdest dream ever.

Chloe was smoking a cigarette when she came into my bedroom wearing clothes that were several sizes too large for her. I was as old as I am now, but even though we're the same age, Chloe looked about fourteen.

"My parents split up," she said, wiping away a tear. Was this a dream or a memory?

"How do you know?" I asked, sitting up in bed and turning on a tiny light on the night table.

The bulb was purple, giving the room a soft, soothing color without jarring us with bright light. I'd been sleeping, and Chloe had been crying, so the eye-friendly bulb was so welcome.

"Well, I heard talk; then my mom has been in her room for about a month," she said slowly, painfully. "I finally asked where my dad was, and that's when she said she didn't know and didn't care." People think rich kids have it easy, but when things go wrong, they almost feel worse. They have all this money, all these connections, and so many resources—what's the use of being privileged if your parents can still fall out of love?

As I thought of asking her if she wanted to lie down with me, she climbed in.

"How are you?" I asked after a few moments of hearts beating in unison.

"I don't know why people can't stay in love," she responded. "None of our friends' parents stay together."

"Everyone's always messing up," I agreed. "Maybe they get married for the wrong reasons. If the foundation is weak, it's gonna crumble eventually."

We lay in bed quietly for a few minutes, listening to the night.

"I usually like the night better than the day," Chloe said. "I feel more . . . myself. But tonight, I feel . . . scared."

"Of what, Clo?" I asked.

"Later," she replied waving it off. "What will I be like when I get older? Will I marry a guy for the wrong reasons?"

That's when I jumped in my sleep and woke up, panicked again about Chloe—both the one who'd left me in that parking lot and the younger one I'd left in my dream. I kept trying to call her, and all I got was voicemail. I can still tell you exactly how it went, right down to the "ums" because I wound up listening to it 800 times over the next seven days while Chloe was off the radar.

"Hi, everybody, it's Chloe! I am getting an *insane* amount of calls right now, so, if you actually are *insane* then, no offense, but please call 911! You can try to leave me a voicemail, but I bet it's filled up. Sooo . . . anyway . . . smile!"

I couldn't help smiling every time just because Chloe told me to.

CHAPTER 5

The 411

IN CASE you were wondering why Chloe's outgoing message made reference to the insane amount of calls she was getting, it was the same reason why I couldn't get a hold of Chloe during the week she disappeared: Simone Westlake.

Simone was a model, actress, and all-around professional fake-rich girl—which means she was pretty much like everyone else we knew. But to be completely honest and not totally complimentary, Simone—an only child who understood the value of being one-of-a-kind—was also like no one else you've ever met. Her father was a South African dry-cleaning magnate who cashed in his (secretly pretty small) stake in his family's chain to make movies. Simone was good at combining both of her father's interests by airing her dirty laundry in "home videos" she and her boy toys liked to make. Simone was leggy and tall, though no one knows exactly *how* tall because she'd never been seen out of pumps since puberty . . . not even in her night-vision skin flicks, filmed strictly for private use, of course.

Her hair was naturally blonde, but she liked to wear it red to contrast her famously emerald-green eyes, which only her closest friends knew were actually an unremarkable shade of wishy-washy hazel. Her eye color was far from the only fake part of Simone. Her real first name was Margaret, her long hair was 95 percent extensions, her nose was sixteen years younger than the rest of Simone, and as for her boobs, I have it on good authority that she took a Polaroid of Chloe's assets to her plastic surgeon and said, "Like these."

Simone was famous for being famous. Chloe wasn't famous for anything yet, so her disappearance wasn't exactly a national news story. Still, it might've attracted more attention except for the fact that a few days before Chloe disappeared, Simone had gotten stoned—aside from a Fendi spy bag, her favorite accessory was a fatty—and accidentally-on-purpose left her cell phone in the gi-normous ladies' room at Caesar's in Las Vegas. Did I say cell phone? Calling the Karat One a cell phone is like calling the Queen Elizabeth 2 a boat. I think it was Simone's beloved "Page Six," the *New York Post* gossip column, that first called it the Billion-Dollar Beeper. In truth, it cost about $45,000, and it was a *lot* more than a beeper. Simone's cell took pictures and videos and could even project movies. It was made of solid gold, unlike Simone's heart. The only thing it couldn't do for Simone was what any of her boyfriends-of-the-moment were there for. Simone loved exclusivity in her gadgets, and only, like, a hundred Karat Ones existed. That meant the Karat One was something you couldn't find just anywhere—except, it turns out, on the vanity in the little girls' room at Caesar's where Simone had left hers.

The next day, when the story broke that all of Simone's many contacts were being swamped with calls and that the dots were connected back to her missing Karat One, Simone told a reporter that some black guy had pushed her over and snatched it—she'd actually used the N-word, but the reporter was her bud and edited her some political correctness. But either way, all of us knew the truth: She'd just left it in the bathroom where she'd been doing lines all night. It was very Simone. For one thing, she lost everything that wasn't attached to her and even some stuff that was—all the cartilage in her nose, for example. And for another, there was a good chance she had every intention of losing that Karat One, realizing the headlines it would grab.

Well, for our group, Simone losing her cell phone was enough of a disaster to warrant celebrity telethons, except all the celebrities were busy dealing with unwanted phone calls. I mean, the entire contents of the cell phone were online, including an adult bookstore's worth of topless self-portraits. Mikela had 464 e-mails the day after Simone lost the Karat One, most of them pictures of guys not wearing any pants. She immediately snapped into action, putting the pictures in different categories: dateable, un-dateable, and question mark. It was like she was playing a reverse game of Hot or Not?

My friend's friend Tia, the big pop singer, got like 2,000 phone calls in about two hours, lots of heavy breathers and death threats. She couldn't take it and went back home to live with her mother in Atlanta. The thing is, she'd never even *met* Simone. Maybe Tia's cell number was one of the basic features of the Karat One.

It was amazing how many people whose numbers were in that cell phone had never even *met* Simone, and couldn't figure out how she'd gotten their numbers in the first place.

Carrie was, of course, the only person who didn't get any calls despite her number being available on 300,000 Web pages. Still, she had her assistant get her a new number because it was the cool thing to do.

I didn't have to worry about it because I had given Simone a fake number. (That poor receptionist at the Equinox Gym!) That incident did make me really paranoid about giving out my number, especially to stoners, and it made Simone even more famous.

Chloe got way more calls than any of us, even though she was probably technically the least famous. People got really nuts with it, calling day and night. I don't know why they picked Chloe. I mean, Simone had all sorts of weirdoes and dignitaries in her Billion-Dollar Beeper—actors, drug dealers, actors who were drug dealers, lesbian cabaret singers, the married mayor of a major city, a famous suck-up reporter . . . my guess is that they called Chloe because she seemed so approachable, normal, and from their galaxy at least, if not from their zip code.

At first, she felt that she needed to be nice to people who called. She'd even ask them questions like, "How are you doing?" and "What's your favorite movie?" even though she should have just told them to get a life.

Not that Chloe had no cojones. One person asked her why she was such an annoying slut. She told the guy to ask his girlfriend. When he said he didn't have one, Chloe just laughed and said, "I know."

Nice.

Eventually, Chloe had to stop answering her phone, and then she stopped taking it with her when she went out. Why didn't she get a new number, a new phone, and a new e-mail right away? I don't know. I guess you just can't always count on drug addicts to be effective at crisis management. Even sober, Chloe wouldn't have known how to change her phone number. It wasn't something she'd ever had to do by herself.

Her phone was missing in action at the same time Chloe was, and it was all Simone's fault.

Exactly seven days after Chloe's disappearance, her divorced parents had teamed up long distance and were considering calling the FBI in on it. They were hesitating because she'd done this kind of thing before. Chloe was like a cat—she would vanish when there was trouble and reappear when things cooled down. Nobody had seen her, but there was a rumor Chip had shown up back at his parents' house, so that probably meant Chloe would surface any day now.

I was with Carrie and Mikela when my cell rang two times in a row. We'd just completed the circuit—Barneys New York on Wilshire, Marni and Fred Segal on Melrose, and The Ivy on Robertson for lunch.

"That is the nicest, craziest, most totally out-there idea I have ever heard," Mikela was saying to Carrie while eyeing Zach Braff and some girl at a corner table—not Mandy Moore! Carrie beamed with pride. All she'd suggested was a welcome-back party for Chloe that she'd never actually go through with.

The first of the two calls came between the crab cakes and the gritted vegetable salad.

I didn't recognize the number, but since everyone had just switched, I couldn't afford to miss anyone good.

"Hello," I said cautiously, disguising my voice to sound like a clerk at Rite Aid just in case it was a *Simple Life* fanatic.

"Nicole. It's Simone." Her voice had that somnambulant quality, half *Stepford* and half Valium.

"Hey, Simone."

"Hey." About thirty seconds of silence ensued, but I was not willing to pull it out of her.

"Okay, anyway, is Chloe there?"

"No, Simone," I said, annoyed that she wasn't aware Chloe was MIA. Mikela and Carrie stopped chewing and pressed their heads to my cell to pick up bits of the conversation.

"Oh," Simone said like a female Andy Warhol. "When you see her, tell her I'm looking for her."

"Simone, *everyone*'s looking for her. That's kind of the point . . . ?" I was losing patience, and my girl posse was giggling.

"Whatever. Tell her to call me if you see her. Later." And with that, she hung up. The dial tone had more personality.

No sooner was that call over than the second call came in. It was from a different number—one I recognized. It was Chloe's home phone. I excitedly picked up. "Chloe? Chloe? Are you okay?"

Chloe sounded a little groggy and a lot sheepish. "Yes, I'm fine, Nicole. Sorry."

It was all she had to say. "Don't worry about it. I'm here with Mik and Carrie, and we're just glad you're all right. You had everyone scared." Our appetizers were cleared virtually untouched, and three matching salads appeared in their place.

"I know, and I'm sorry," Chloe continued. "I was wondering if just you and I could meet for coffee at our place. Like . . . tomorrow at noon? I think I need to ask your, um, advice about some things."

I was so relieved. This sounded like, literally, a call for help.

"You got it, girl. I'll be there. Just me," I glanced at

Mikela and Carrie, who had gone from exchanging relieved glances to attacking their salads and pretending not
to eavesdrop on every single word I was saying.

Chloe was alive. Now it was up to me to try to get her
some help.

Out of the Frying Pan

I COULD ALWAYS TELL when Chloe was wasted. It wasn't just about spazzy behavior—this being L.A., it was also about wardrobe choices. Instead of being her regular fashion-forward self, she would dress really, really preppy. I'm no shrink, but I think it was like she wanted to make up for being a junkie by looking like a twenty-three-year-old soccer mom.

The day after her sudden return, at "our place"—the Malibu Coffee Bean near where we'd survived high school together—she was rockin' a pink Lacoste polo, white capris, plaid canvas sneaks, and pigtails. No doubt about it, Chloe was using.

"I can't believe the most coverage I've ever gotten in the celebrity mags is pictures of me looking so busted," she lamented. She was disgustedly paging through a stack of magazines, letting out a little screech every time she saw a grotesque picture of herself from the Mode incident. She was so engrossed in how nasty she'd looked that night and in calculating how many readers would think the same thing that she kept "forgetting" to tell me what had gone on during her absence.

"I looked so brutal that night," she kept saying over and over again, touching her nose as if to make sure it was still attached. "I can't believe I looked as bad as I felt."

When you grow up in Bel Air and shop only in expensive boutiques on Rodeo and Robertson, you develop a kind of allergy to anything unpretty—clothes, cars . . . even people. It's awful, I now know, and I do hate to admit it, but you start thinking that if you hang around unattractive people, their homeliness can be contagious. Totally shallow, but that's the way it was. Growing up, Chloe and I used to wonder why anyone would ever *choose* to be fat or ugly. For our community service project in high school, Chloe even suggested starting a fund for poor teens who couldn't afford plastic surgery—and she was serious. I think we could've raised $50,000 just from our classmates if the teachers hadn't put a stop to it.

Now, it was Chloe who needed help. Aside from her Izod costume, her skin, usually a warm caramel, was all pale and gluey, and her raccoon eyes were blinking a mile a minute. If she'd looked in the mirror, she would have seen one of those zombies from *Dawn of the Dead* staring back at her. I knew the look because that used to be me. As

I sipped a raspberry tea, I wanted to tell her I knew what was going on . . . but I couldn't. Or maybe I didn't really want to risk pushing her away. I mean, I was just glad she was *alive* after what I'd witnessed. She didn't even have a black eye—I figured it must be because Chip hit like a girl.

"Clo, you were . . . Out. Of. Control," I told her sternly. "It's not about your appearance. This is not *America's Next Top Model.*"

"I'm sorry you had to see that," she told me, pigtails bouncing. "I was a little crazy, I guess. Honestly . . . I don't remember it much."

It was her way of apologizing, like if she explained away her behavior with craziness, I'd just forget about it. But the thing was, I wasn't *angry*, even though I almost got run over, and there were plenty of pictures of *me* in those tabloids, too, standing around looking like a Venice Beach vendor caught in the headlights. But I wasn't worried about my image; I was more worried about what Chloe was actually becoming.

"I'll paint a picture," I told her. "First, you Jackie Chan none other than Ana Cannon in a club. Then your boyfriend bitch-slaps you. Then you do some idiotic break dancing move in the most vile puddle of water in all of Hollywood and peel away while I'm screaming your name. Click-click-click." I snapped my fingers to simulate the paparazzi capturing every moment on film. "Then I call you every hour on the hour and only get your voicemail."

The whole incident had replaced Chloe's notorious hunger strike as her most embarrassing public display. A few months earlier, drunk out of her mind, Chloe was craving a sandwich so desperately, and yet everyone refused to take her to IHOP. So she'd walked out into the middle of the street at Hollywood and Vine and had lain down in protest. She didn't get hit by a car and Joey had plopped down right next to her in solidarity, so it could have been worse—but it had seemed pretty untoppable as a moment of shame at the time.

"I know; I know." She seemed distantly remorseful. Sorta like she knew she should be embarrassed but didn't really have it in her. Drugs don't let you feel emotions. "My dress is totally wrecked after all that," she noted ruefully. I guess Ana's really *is* one-of-a-kind now." Then she brightened. "I think mine might actually look better all torn up!"

"Chloe, you can't just keep . . ."

"Oh, and I got a new cell!" She pulled it out to prove it, and, as if on cue, it rang. She looked surprised, put up a finger, looked to see who it was, and answered. Then she mouthed "Simone," shrugged an apology, got up, and wandered off. Simone. The very reason I'd spent seven days wondering if Chloe was dead or alive. "Oh, by the way, Simone is looking for you," had somehow never escaped my lips once I'd seen Chloe. Sue me—I'm a terrible social secretary.

I'm sure Chloe really *didn't* remember where she'd stayed that week. Maybe she'd spent the whole time terrified; maybe she was having as much fun as a clotheshorse like me let loose in a Zac Posen showroom. I was guessing she'd never know and that neither would I—drugs are like that sometimes. But *I* remember a *lot* from that week, and let me tell you, it sucked. I couldn't sleep. I couldn't eat. I couldn't even shop. Actually that's not true: I *had* gotten this amazing Marni backless dress at Barneys the day before—but I didn't really go crazy like normal.

I also had that creepy dream over and over again.

Ironically, it was Simone who was calling now and interrupting my one chance to talk some sense into Chloe. Worse, Simone was in the process of making Chloe an offer she couldn't refuse—and one that was going to change Chloe's life forever.

Okay, part of me was glad that we'd been interrupted. I'm not good at that sort of stuff, and anyway, if she was ready to change . . . well, I'm not sure there really was much *anyone* could say to force the issue.

I sat waiting, making my tea disappear, wondering whether I was finally going to perform a one-woman intervention.

Chloe finally bye-byed Simone and returned to our table. She just stood there for a minute looking shocked.

"What, Chloe? What is it?" Like all Virgos, I'm not known for my patience.

A smile crept up Chloe's face like a delayed reaction, and she seemed stunned sober for a minute. "Guess what? Simone is going to make me famous."

"What for?" I asked.

Chloe laughed and sat down, her eyes widening. "You know how Magdalena always picks spokesmodels who are, like, supposed to be the new It girls?"

Magdalena Cosmetics was second only to MAC and was known for choosing girls on the brink of stardom to hawk their high-end makeup to mall rats, movie stars, men in drag, and moms. Their shades invented cute-name syndrome, with tags like "Swallowed Canary Yellow." Everyone knew that *any* girl chosen to be the painted face of Magdalena would get magazine spreads, movie contracts, and late-night talk show jabs. That gig was like the crack of fame.

"Uh, *yeah*," I duhhed her. "They're choosing *Simone*?"

"Yes, but this time they're choosing two best friends— it's the first time ever!—and Simone wants me to be the best friend." She stared at me with a goofy grin.

"How nice that Simone has casting approval over who her best friend is," I said. "And you hardly even *wear* makeup."

Just then, Carrie's face invaded our space from over my left shoulder. Like a dog hearing a bag of Fritos being opened somewhere in the vicinity, she was *right there*.

"Oh, my God, Chloe, that is *so amazing!*" she cooed. "You're so lucky! You *totally* deserve it. But you are so lucky!" Carrie sat down in the chair between us and hugged Chloe hysterically. Obviously, she'd caught the location of our just-us meeting the day before. I wondered if Mikela would be next, but then I remembered Mikela was doing a David LaChapelle shoot for *W*, which kind of trumped any passing interest she might have in Chloe's personal or professional—would they ever be separate again?—life.

Chloe and I kind of rolled our eyes at each other—we both knew Carrie would be glued to her from then on in if it meant she might be able to force her way into any screen time.

"Thanks!" Chloe chirped, beginning to fuzz out. Right in front of us, she popped a Xanax and washed it down with an iced latte.

"Yeah, Chloe," I said unenthusiastically. "What can I say? This *is* the biggest break ever."

"'Glamour, parties, friendship,'" Chloe said like she was reciting the lines from a school play. "That's their theme this season."

"Is that in order?" I asked, and Carrie scowled at me.

"Anyway, the best part is that they're doing this sort of as a reality show—they're going to follow us around with cameras and film everything we do together. The commercials are going to be like a minute or two minutes long, all over MTV and everywhere else, and they'll be, like, mini-documentaries."

Carrie squealed, which didn't surprise me, considering her history—she'd slept with the most grotesque elephant in the history of reality television, just because he was famous. Chloe was lucky she wasn't a guy or she'd be next on Carrie's list.

"Chloe," I reasoned. "You haven't spent a day with Simone in a year or more. She's always busy with other friends. Don't feel like I'm killing your buzz, but what reality is there to show?"

After one of those long, druggy pauses you had to get used to if you were friends with an addict, she said, "Honestly . . .

I don't really remember all the details of what she said, but she said she talked with the Magdalena people, and they want me for sure. I think they're going to take us on a promo tour together? We'll spend lots of time together." It dawned on Chloe that I wasn't as excited as she and Carrie were. "And anyway," she said defensively, "it doesn't really seem like that hard of a decision. I *do* hang out with Simone and go to parties. It won't be that different from my regular life, only that it will be with camera crews and lots of free makeup. I think it pays unbelievably. Don't you get it, Nicole? I'm sick of being like Brittany Murphy in *Uptown Girls*—I want to have a purpose. Even if it's only for the next few weeks."

"Sorry, Chloe. I hear you. Congratulations, girl." I leaned across Carrie and gave Chloe the reassuring hug she craved at that moment. We finished our drinks, abandoned Carrie to hers (she was undoubtedly calling everyone to tell them the news for Chloe), and walked to the parking lot. I kissed her on the cheek and watched her climb into her mom's black BMW. She took off down the hill to the Pacific Coast Highway, right into the fast lane.

That's when I remembered part of the reason I'd been so desperate to see Chloe—I still had her diamond earring in my bag. How could she not realize it was missing? It was from her dad and worth more than the car she was driving, but probably it was safer with me than it was in that car anyway—as she hit the PCH, she nearly hit a Mini-Cooper.

She had just returned from being MIA. Why did I get the feeling Chloe Parker was about to disappear again?

CHAPTER 7

The Legend of Simone Westlake

CHLOE, MIKELA, Carrie, Joey, Lanny, and I convened one sultry evening not long after around a poolside table at Tropicana Bar in the Roosevelt, the newest in spot that a year earlier had been cabana non grata—it used to be kind of sketchy, a nothing lounge in the quaint old Hollywood and Highland hotel where the first Academy Awards had been held in the 1920s. Seemingly overnight, the bar and the entire hotel had been lifestyle produced into fabulous mid-century modern masterpieces where every late-century modern scenester was dying to be seen. Everywhere you looked there was chrome, flip-flops, and hot-looking guys and girls. Of course, beauty is only skin deep, and like the amazing pool with its David Hockney mural illuminated under a glass-still surface, our transparent table definitely had a shallow end—our hostess, Simone Westlake.

Simone had invited us all to hang out and chat about the fabulous TV opportunity *she* was allowing Chloe to share in. At first, I thought she was just going to brag. But as the drinks kept coming, I realized Simone was also giving us all fair warning that since we were so central to Chloe's life, we may be in the line of fire. See, Simone isn't Einstein, but it would be a mistake to underestimate her. In fact, Simone Westlake wasn't even four years old and still living down in San Diego when she killed her tutor.

This is kind of an urban legend among our crowd— you know, like the lady who brought back the Chihuahua from Mexico though it turned out to be a rat? This story also has a legendary rat in it, but I'm pretty sure it's true.

According to Elsa, the imposing, was-she-once-a guy? Westlake housekeeper, twenty years earlier, she had been hired after the death of an elderly woman named Ilsa who'd been found spreadeagled in the family's veranda. Ilsa had apparently decomposed there for twenty-four hours before the gardener arrived and lodged the most understandable "not in my job description" protest of all time.

The last time Ilsa had been seen alive, she was going over the alphabet with little Simone, who was bored and never much cared for tutoring—pre-or-post-K. Simone didn't like Ilsa because Ilsa had told on her for using her mother's vintage Birkin bag for her Barbie dolls, and Ilsa didn't like Simone because Ilsa was phobic of being up so high on Simone's balcony, the only place Simone would agree to sit still and learn.

When Ilsa failed to show up for work the day after she'd spent time standing on that dreaded balcony, throwing a three-going-on-four-year old Simone in the air while she squealed in delight, Simone's mother was complaining on the phone about the scarcity of good help. Little Simone said earnestly, "Ilsa isn't missing, Mommy. She's been sleeping down on the veranda outside my window since yesterday." Ilsa the tutor had learned a valuable lesson the hard way: There is no beating sense into Simone's head.

Elsa told Chloe—whom she'd always thought of as a good influence on Simone—that the little girl's *Bad Seed* episode was never fully explained and that Simone seemed unbothered by it. Not long after, Simone's dad, Terence, sold his business and moved to L.A. to make movies and wound up living right next door to the Parkers. That move helped minimize any gossip about the incident, and the Elsa/Ilsa confusion meant lots of people thought the Westlakes had never switched housekeepers at all. Even Simone sometimes forgot the two were different people. She remembered whenever she tried to backtalk Elsa because Elsa was one domestic with the powerful personality and physical brawn to keep Simone Westlake in line.

"You guys, this show is going to be awesome," Simone announced over the rim of her drink. She always had that druggy, trance-like way of speaking that was somehow a little mesmerizing—not in a fascinating way, more like you were being hypnotized. She wore a flaming orange wrap dress that was like an exclamation point in the room—somehow, no one else for miles was in orange, as if Simone had managed to call ahead.

"Yes," Chloe agreed, manic on coke, "it's going to be . . . so big."

"Hey, I thought it was a commercial, not a show," Lanny interjected. I was glad he was able to read my mind.

"It's not a *commercial*," Simone sneered. "God, it's more than that. Magdalena is going to film a lot of our . . . like . . . *lives*. If you're on camera that much, you're eventually going to get superfamous."

"Even if they just used the same commercial over and over on MTV, you'd probably get lots of exposure," Mikela pointed out. It was the middle of the night, and she was sitting in public in a white bikini with stilettos. Mikela knew about exposure.

"It's not a *commercial*," Simone insisted. "The way they're describing it to me, they'll film some stuff of us doing our normal things, like, candid stuff. Then they'll film us in these situations they come up with. Like, I don't know, there's talk of a mall tour or whatever. And maybe they'll have us wearing the makeup and doing a runway show or something. It'll be fletch." She was still trying to make "fletch" happen. She was good about stealing lines from movies, rappers, her BFFs—and then taking all the credit for inventing them.

"I can't really see you guys in a mall," Joey snorted, running his hand through his long hair. Chloe's face darkened—anything critical Joey ever said was ten times harsher than if someone else had said it. Would she ever get over him? Sensing his asshole status through a heroin haze, Joey smiled at Chloe and quickly made it right. "But as soon as America sees you guys on TV, I'm sure you'll be the new Mary Kate and Ashley." Chloe liked that and toasted the sentiment solo.

"Besides," Simone continued, "it *will* be a show. I don't believe they're going to spend all that money on a few commercials. Once people see me on TV, I'll make sure they want more."

"Don't forget about Chloe, Simone," I said, probably a little crisply. Hiding my true feelings is not my strong suit.

Overcompensating, Simone gave me the world's most awkward half-hug and darlinged me and said, "No, yeah, Chloe, too. Really, all of you guys."

The table was silent while all of us chewed on this last tidbit, wondering to ourselves where our six-figure con-tracts were if we were going to be a part of this venture. I had the perfect out. "Well, I'm under contract to FOX, so I doubt they'll sign off on me being in it."

"Yeah, Magdalena knows that," Simone said, "but everyone else will be, you know, caught on tape."

"Oh, definitely!" Carrie said a little too quickly. "I mean, even if we're not *trying* to be, we're *always* around Chloe. And you. So of course we'll be in some of the footage."

Simone reached into her big Louis V bag and pulled out a stack of papers. Turns out they were more like documents—she had one for all of us, including me, and they were all waivers stating that we gave permission to have ourselves filmed in natural circumstances by Magdalena and that the footage was fair game to be inserted into their national advertising campaign. Chloe didn't get one since she would be getting a more far-reaching contract. Good thing, since she was in and out of awareness. She snapped back in when I told Simone I had no intention of signing anything.

"I just told you I can't participate," I said. "I could get sued."

Simone was ready for me. "No, seriously, just read it, it's like a page long. It says on yours that you don't consent to anything being aired without final approval and stuff. That way, if you happen to be around, they don't have to waste time filming around you. It's no big deal. It's for Chloe."

"Yeah, Nicole, come *onnn!*" Chloe pleaded. "I don't wanna make waves with them when things aren't even final yet. What if Magdalena backs out because my friends aren't being cool?"

As Chloe was giving me seal eyes, Simone was giving me a ball point pen. I looked around the table. Lanny and Joey were signing without much concern, and Mikela and Carrie had already signed. I think Carrie had signed hers midair.

"Please, Nicole?" It was always hard to say no to Clo.

"I'll show it to my manager," I said. "I at least have to do that. If she's okay with it, I'll sign. Okay?"

Chloe beamed. "Deal."

Before we could get back to less weird conversation, a Simone look-alike timidly stepped up to her and professed undying love. Simone wasn't all *that* famous then, but she was known. Already E! had discovered her in its clip shows, and she'd done a tarty ad campaign for Dress, a clothier who paid her an average person's annual salary to say, "Now *that's* a Dress!" in an annoying thirty-second spot. Obviously, this girl had seen it.

"Could we do a picture together?" she finally asked.

"Sure," Simone said, all about the fans even before she had any. The girl got between Simone and Chloe in a way I wished I could, and Lanny helpfully cell phone–snapped a pic of the three of them. We passed the phone around and had a look, even though the real deals were sitting right there, flesh and blood, right in front of our faces.

"We look hot," Simone cooed. "Thanks." Who had done whom the favor? Chloe put her arm around Simone like they were born-again best friends, and they linked elbows, drinking from each other's glasses. It was funny even to me, and all of us laughed loudly, probably making the other patrons wonder what the joke was and how to get in on it.

Seeing Chloe and Simone interacting reminded me of their history. I shouldn't have been so surprised that they had chemistry, even if it did piss me off.

Chloe and her next-door neighbor Simone had forged a friendship at Hartley, their superexclusive prep school. Even if you'd seen them in their uniforms you'd have been able to tell how different they were. Whoever said that school uniforms are identical knows nothing about girls. Underneath her blue or gray skirt and white shirt, Chloe normally wore pink tights or a leotard and different color shoes like Punky Brewster, an early role model. Simone wore g-strings and platforms and accessorized with a Lolita lollipop. You weren't supposed to have food, especially candy, in class, but all the male teachers would let Simone have her suckers because she made this big thing about licking them seductively. These are the same men who today spend their time cruising the Internet for barely-legal porn.

On play dates, Simone would show up in a micromini and a halter, holding a plastic pail for the sand box. She didn't wear makeup. Until fourth grade. Chloe, however, wore gingham bib-style dresses that went down to her ankles and black-and-white Mary Janes. You could tell whose mother was paying attention and whose wasn't.

As different as they were deep down, Chloe and Simone actually had a lot in common, mainly that they both got bored really easily in school. They were always laughing at everything—their parents, their pets, their teachers' clothes. If there was nothing to laugh at, they'd laugh at that, too. They loved dancing. When their mothers were still talking, they'd take the girls to the Beverly Center, where they'd create elaborate dance routines on the escalators, one going up, one going down.

As we devoured cocktails and dished at the Tropicana that night, it was obvious to everyone there that Chloe and Simone were both on their way up professionally—but personally, both were heading in the opposite direction. Before all of us left, they girl-trekked to the bathroom together, and it wasn't to check their makeup.

The Art of
the Deal

ASTRID DILLINGER was a career woman and a study in contradictions—she made a bundle of money but never splurged, she wore tasteful Donna Karan suits with Costco pantyhose, she worked for the country's coolest beauty products manufacturer, and yet she never spent any time beautifying *herself*. Her dark hair was pulled back into an unfun bun, her eyes were only defined from the rest of her face by their dark brown irises, and she was possibly the last anti-tooth whitening hold-out in the greater Los Angeles area. But that was okay—no one ever saw her smile.

I was sitting with Astrid around a gigantic conference table in a wall-to-wall lavender room inside a glass office building so close to Robertson Boulevard—and yet so far away. How did I get myself into that situation in the first place? I wasn't the one with the advertising deal, and my manager had been down on the idea of agreeing to be filmed under the assumption that most of it wouldn't be used, since if most of it wouldn't be used, most of it shouldn't be filmed in the first place. But Chloe had text me an urgent plea to come hold her hand while she signed her deal with Magdalena before we could go off to lunch at Koi for a little sushibration, and I'd dutifully shown up, provided I.D., and been escorted so many floors up that we'd never get out if a big earthquake hit. Astrid had been my greeter.

"I handle promotion," she told me. "I also oversee advertising, direct human resources, and have my hand in product testing." Was I in New York? Because this woman was so tightly wound up, I thought she might strike noon at twelve o'clock. "I do a lot. I have a lot of responsibility," she continued, enunciating each syllable of the word like it were a sentence unto itself. "And it has come to my attention that you are wavering on the waiver. Don't you want your friend to be famous like you? Is this a jealousy thing?" She actually made a little hissing cat noise and raked imaginary claws at me with her blunted fingernails.

I couldn't help but laugh. I just could not take her seriously. "No, no, nothing like that," I said. "I just have to protect myself. I'm sure Magdalena means the best."

"Oh, she does," Astrid said solemnly. I was noticing that in the corporate headquarters, "Magdalena" was used interchangeably to refer both to the company and to the larger-than-life woman who founded it. As if on cue, the doors to the conference room were thrown open, and

Magdalena herself strode in with Chloe on one arm and Simone on the other. About twenty people were following a few, respectful paces behind. They appeared to be a mix of lawyers, accountants, administrative assistants, and perhaps a stray gigolo or two.

"We are not going to make *history*," Magdalena announced to no one and everyone. "We are going to make *future*. Astrid—write that one down! That was good. Why can't you think of things like that?"

Astrid had already written it down, virtually shorthanding it as Magdalena spoke. I've grown up around Hollywood superstars, and I've seen my fair share of eccentrics. Michael Jackson is my godfather. But Magdalena sort of blew me away. From the neck down, she looked about thirty—she had an hourglass figure like women used to have. Think prehistoric Raquel Welch. She was distastefully but expensively clad in a lavender suit and skirt that appeared to be not only custom-made for her but also sewn directly onto her body. But it's a good thing her eyes were in her head because you couldn't help staring at that face—she appeared to have tried, oh, *everything* to stay looking young, and instead of having the desired effect, the end result was that she looked like a stuffed animal. Her cheeks were bulbous, her lips so plump they barely touched, and her eyes were stretched feline under lash extensions. A little makeup never hurt anyone, but a *lot* of makeup sure had—she seemed to be wearing every product her company manufactured all at once. Her hair was an eerily unnatural rust color, tortured into a helmet suitable for riding a motorcycle on the highway.

"Simone, Chloe, I see your friend is here—lovely to see you, Nicole." Magdalena pronounced my name "NEEcole," and her accent changed from French to Hungarian to you're-just-makin'-that-up from line to line. She kissed my cheek, and I thought I'd smell like lavender for a month.

"It's nice to meet you," I said in a small voice, awed by the calamity of her presence. I cut my eyes at Chloe, mouthing that I would kill her later.

That's when I realized that after the twenty hangers-on, another handful of people were still entering the room—and they were headed up by a guy holding a professional video camera and a serious young girl whispering into his ear, directing him on who, what, and where to film. Yes, there was a video crew. Already. And I was already being filmed.

"Chloe, did you not get my message?" I asked her sweetly. Just in case, I figured it wouldn't pay to throw a fit on tape.

Chloe sat next to me, grabbing my hand and imploring me with her bloodshot eyes. Magdalena sat at the head of the table as if she were perching on a throne, and the cameras swirled around her, Simone, Chloe, and finally me.

"Nicole, we are so grateful you'll sign our contract," Magdalena said through a smile. "It means the world to us. And it means the deal for Simone and Chloe. Of course, we're hiring them for their own fabulous selves, and you'll *hardly* be involved. But we do need to cross our Is and dot our Ts." No one corrected her.

"Well, actually . . ." I said. It's kind of hard to think when the lens of a camera is pressed literally to the side of your face. Not only were there legal issues with the arrangement, it really wouldn't have been good for my image to be associated with the likes of Simone.

"I've got your waiver right here," Astrid said, and believe me, she did. It was out, and a pen was poised in her hand just as firmly as if it were sticking out of a desk set. I looked at everyone; everyone looked at me. I thought about Chloe's child-like desire to succeed and be loved. I weighed it all against *my* desire to see Simone denied *something* in her life. And I signed. It was only TV ads, and I would probably barely be in them, right? I'd just be background ambience.

As soon as I'd caved, the attention went off me and back onto Chloe and Simone, with the cameras filming them signing their contracts with big smiles and inside jokes and, wow—they were practically doing each other's hair.

"You're definitely the closest friends I've ever seen," Magdalena observed. How she could see out of those eyelashes was a big mystery.

"We've *always* been *best, best* friends," Simone said. I bristled, but only internally—I didn't want to wind up as a subplot in the ads.

While we were all seated at this crazy-long boardroom table, yes-men and yes-women began telling Simone and Chloe everything that they would be doing. They both got so amazingly bored, it wasn't even funny. Chloe ordered two shots of Patrón tequila like she was in a bar.

Chloe practically fell asleep during some guy's Power-Point presentation about their future appearances while Simone played with her gum and had text-message sex with some guy on her pager—at least that's what Chloe figured Simone was doing because she kept typing "o god o god o god" over and over again. I just wished the guy could have seen how bored to within an inch of her life she was while she was supposedly in orgasmic heaven.

From what Chloe and I could tell, the idea was that Chloe and Simone would be going around the country to store openings and events. Pretty much every moment would be taped and could be broadcast in any medium in lengths of 30, 60, 90 or 120 seconds.

"We aren't just selling lip liner, girls," said Astrid. "We are selling lifestyle—*your* lifestyle. The boys, the clothes, the in-jokes: We're looking for the whole kit and caboodle."

The last time anyone sold a "kit and caboodle" was probably the 1870s, but we got the picture.

They showed us a dummied-up life-sized cutout of the two of them that had been made from event photos, just to give us an idea of some of their marketing plans. Chloe looked closely at the eyes in her picture and wondered how obvious it was that she was so insanely dopesick it was ridiculous. She remembered squirting a river of Visine in them to make them less bloodshot the night that picture had been snapped, but it hadn't really helped. She looked to me like she was wondering, "Do I really look like this . . . all the time?"

"We were able to digitize your eyes, so they weren't so red," Astrid whispered in her ear, leaning across my lap somewhat invasively. It was like Astrid was firing a warning shot.

"I noticed you didn't have the computer do anything with my nipples," Chloe responded under her breath. "I didn't know I was so cold that day."

"Let's show the girls some of our goodies," Magdalena said, recapturing control of the powwow. I had this image of RuPaul untaping himself down there as she said this, so I was really hoping she meant food or something a little more appetizing.

Suddenly, some of the suits started folding up a wall, and the huge room got huger—and was filled with light. In a hidden niche was an entire planet's worth of spotlit Magdalena products, more product than Simone and Chloe had ever laid eyes on combined. Seeing a warehouse of cute shoes? That would make me hot. Seeing a ton of beauty aides? Honestly, it was kind of scary.

I mean, there were eleven different kinds of leave-in conditioner and thirty-three shades of matte red lipstick. There were gallons of creams and sunscreen and enough polish to cover all the nails of all the people that Chloe had ever met, and probably their kids' nails and their kid's kids' nails, too.

"Wow, there's so much product here it's *retarded*," said Simone.

Astrid immediately pronounced, "We would prefer you didn't use that word."

"Is that because regular people don't know what 'product' is?" Simone asked.

No one answered her.

Chloe, though, was far from loving it. The sight of all that shiny makeup and all those bottles of sudsy junk freaked her out worse than it did me. Chloe always felt that besides prom and the Golden Globes, makeup just should *not* be that big a part of a girl's life—it wasn't for her. Chloe was the quintessential skin and sunshine girl, and all that junk just felt like having clay all over her face. Chloe was the kind of girl who would rub her eyes and not worry about smearing anything—she was fashion-forward, but clean. But she was going to be paid for it, so she didn't complain. To be polite, she even asked if she could have a little powder.

Simone was different. She wore makeup all day long, every day, and once said that makeup was the one thing that distinguished people from animals. She never left home without her face done. Needless to say, she responded to the sight of all that product by trying to stuff as much of it as she possibly could into her candy-colored Louis V.

As she did, some suits went on about how they had all these different lines—a sports line for cheerleaders and beach volleyball players; a school line with names like "Phys Red," "Blackboard," and "Schoolbus Orange;" an urban line for black girls and black-wannabes where the colors were named after different subway lines in New York.

They were told they would be wearing all of it "in the field," doing stuff to demonstrate the "Magdalena lifestyle in action."

Exciting words, but in the board*room*, everything sounds bor*ing*.

It became so obvious how much Chloe and Simone were not paying attention that Astrid decided to direct the cameras to really focus on the girls' reactions, which of course livened them right up.

I noticed the camera's fixation with Simone. She was wearing a strappy, sky-blue Chloé dress. It wasn't something you'd wear to a business meeting or randomly during the day even. I couldn't be sure, but I felt like she'd known all along this whole thing would be filmed, and I *knew* Chloe hadn't been informed because she was clearly more than a little chemically imbalanced. It wasn't enough that it would read on TV, but it wasn't ideal.

Part of the reason Simone always looked chic was her personal stylist, Brittany, the most in-demand image-maker among the A-list. Simone was still B-list, but she'd discovered Brittany and had become her walking billboard. Actually, she didn't exactly discover Brittany.

A year earlier, Ashton Kutcher, who knew Mikela from his B.D. (before Demi) days, had been talked into pranking Simone on *Punk'd*. The gag was that Simone was going to be working with a new stylist on a Dress shoot . . . except the stylist was actually a thirteen-year-old Los Feliz middle-schooler with no experience in fashion. The plan was that Simone would flip out, and Mikela would get to punk her for all time. She probably wouldn't be mad since it would be great exposure.

Instead, Simone found she was on the same wavelength with the adolescent, who was just pulling fashion advice out of her ass. "Do I look good in this yellow one?" Simone asked, holding a Dress creation up to herself.

"Mmmm . . . no," Brittany said, assessing her with a kid's shrug. "Yellow is gay. You should do white. No one is wearing that right now. And here, take my Hello Kitty earrings. They're pierced, but we can just wash them."

Simone had pondered this for a moment, then said, "'Kay, thanks. Should I wear your wristband, too?" It was a ratty black MADE band, and she wore it mid-bicep.

Simone wasn't mad at Mikela when the bullshit hit the fan—she was grateful for being inadvertently introduced to her style muse, a kid who hadn't gotten her period yet. It was the first time Ashton himself got punked, and the episode never aired, but the Dress ad helped introduce a Simone look that was instantly copied by everyone but me. She'd never heard of any famous designers except Joel and Benji Madden, but precocious Brittany was suddenly in demand as a stylist. She later emancipated herself with Terence Westlake's lawyer's assistance and even opened a boutique out of her new Malibu bachelorette pad.

If Simone had planned to be filmed that afternoon we spent in the boardroom, it wouldn't have been the first thing staged for "reality" TV.

"We're almost famous already," Simone said blankly. It sounded dumb, but it also sounded like a perfect sound-bite, one that would wind up in the finished commercials.

"Did makeup ever make anyone famous?" Chloe asked giddily. Simone looked visibly disgruntled that Chloe had one-upped her in the soundbite department.

Magdalena cleared her throat. "*Hello!*" she said, and she was the first senior citizen I'd ever heard say it that way. Everyone laughed politely.

I felt like I saw the producer gesturing to Chloe, and right afterward Chloe asked me if I was happy for her. The conversation began to feel scripted, except I was the only one improvising. Thing is, if everyone knows exactly what to say except for one person, there are only a few likely possibilities for what that person will say or do anyway.

"Yes, Clo. I'm very happy for you. Congrats."

Hardly skipping a beat, Chloe turned to Simone. "We're going to Koi after—wanna come?"

"Yeah, that would rock," Simone said.

I discreetly excused myself and found the ladies' room, which was like a palace of lavender marble. It truly was . . . something. It hardly felt like the appropriate place to do the things normally associated with a bathroom, especially since the doors to the stalls were this freaky transparent glass that would magically fog up, translucent only when they were shut. I decided I'd just powder my face a bit. If I was going to be filmed, there was no good reason to be shiny. Mid-powder, Chloe came in, reflexively reaching into her bag for what I felt sure was her gak sack. But she'd never done drugs in front of me (she'd only been wasted *on* drugs in front of me), so she stopped short when she realized that this was where I'd disappeared to.

"Can you believe it?" she said, joining me at the sink. She fumbled with her clutch, fishing around inside. Ironically, she was having a hard time unearthing any prop makeup, and she was *at* the Magdalena headquarters.

"No," I said. "But also, yes. I can. Everyone's always known you were a little star. Now you'll be a big one."

"Thanks, Nicole," she said a little too emphatically, her system coked and stoked. "I really appreciate that you signed the papers. I'm sure it won't be too . . . invasive."

As she spoke, the bathroom door crept open, and Astrid peered around it. Her spider eyes fixed on us momentarily, then she stepped into the room, allowing the camera crew to silently enter behind her. Chloe trailed off as they approached and fanned out in a semi-circle. Someone lowered a boom mike between us from above. We looked at each other, then at Astrid, and then at the nameless young producer girl with our best "Are you kidding me?" faces.

Astrid inhaled the perfumed air and said to us as if she were being fined $1,000 for every word she had to speak, "It's in the contract."

Chloe turned back to me, looking slightly bewildered and more than a bit scared.

CHAPTER **9**

Fish Tale

I F YOU'VE NEVER BEEN TO KOI, Japanese heaven on North La Cienega, I'd recommend the crab handroll followed by the crispy tuna and the spicy seared albacore with crispy onions. You can't go wrong in that place—they've really figured out ways to work magic with fish.

Chloe was like Koi in that she figured out long ago countless ways to make simple things simply amazing. For example, she made all of our group hang-outs seem like clandestine rendezvous. All of us felt like we were included in some kind of secret, like everyone was looking at us and wondering what was going on. Partly this could be written off to her slightly bombastic behavior—she knew how to grab attention without trying, just by letting herself laugh out loud or by dancing on a chair to crack us up.

But Simone knew how to direct attention like a traffic

cop handling rush hour, so it shouldn't have surprised me when our big, friendly lunch at Koi turned into a big, unfriendly melodrama.

The good news is that when I walked into the room, the entire gang was there including both Chloe and Simone, but that the Magdalena crew had not yet arrived—yes, they were filming this, too. With his usual impeccable timing, Joey had brought along this Russian girl he'd been dating, a user (in more ways than one) named Natasha, the daughter of a hotelier and a particularly exotic piece of arm candy whose czarina air couldn't have been more perfect to give Chloe room for self-doubt. Natasha was okay, but I didn't believe her hype.

I took my seat midsentence.

"—and they filmed everything, everything. They even followed us into the bathroom, right Nicole?"

I raised my eyebrows in confirmation.

Carrie was beside herself with jealousy, then began to study her reflection in the mirror behind our table. After all, cameras were en route.

"It sounds great," Joey said, "but a little intimidating. I couldn't do it."

"Of course *you* couldn't do it," Lanny teased him. "Imagine what they'd catch you doing." Natasha's stare kept Joey from smiling too broadly. But Lanny had reminded us all—including Chloe—that the cameras could catch unflattering things, whether they were used in the commercials or passed around among gossip columnists.

"They won't catch me doing anything I don't want them to," Simone vowed. I, for one, believed her.

"Yeah," Chloe said a little distantly. I could see the wheels in her head turning. Mine were turning, too.

"I think the whole thing is a bit vulgar—very American," Natasha said dismissively around bites of cucumber salad. She ate like a cat would, slowly, intently, and with ferocious grace. "To have everything filmed! They would have to pay me hundreds of thousands of dollars."

Chloe looked like cold water had been thrown in her face, and I'm sure that would have been a good idea.

"They are," Simone said, sipping her green tea. She said it very matter-of-factly. She was good at getting a point across almost before you saw it on the horizon.

Natasha's eyes widened. There would be no more cracks from her.

"That's a *lot* of sushi," Lanny said. "Just don't let your guard down."

"You should have Joey do a song, like, an instrumental in the background," Mikela suggested. Joey waved off that idea with a scowl.

"Yeah, right," he said. "I haven't done anything good in a long time. Plus they probably have a deal with Death Cab for Cutie or something."

Astrid cell phoned Simone to let her know they were pulling up. Already, Simone was chummy with the person at Magdalena who would probably be making most of the editing decisions.

"Before they get here," Chloe said, smiling proudly. "I wanted to say something." All of us waited for a little joke or maybe one more toast. Instead, Chloe's lip trembled as she announced, "I'm going clean for the whole time we film."

Joey broke the pregnant silence first with a derisive snort. Natasha rolled her eyes. Carrie was still all up in the mirror, but Mikela beside her nudged Chloe, with a nonverbal "aw, c'mon." Lanny looked mortified and averted his gaze.

I just stared at her.

Chloe turned to take in each of our faces, her mouth tightening with anger with each new insult. It was clear that her proclamation was being taken very lightly. The fact that none of us meant to hurt her made it all the more hurtful because our reactions were so spontaneous.

In that moment, I wanted to tell her how happy I was to hear that. I could still salvage some of my intervention speech, even if it *were* going to be after the fact. But something made me feel like she wasn't really being real just yet. Her words rang hollow. And before I could open my mouth, Simone shamed us all by speaking first.

"I think that's really cool, Chloe," she said. "It sounds like a good idea. Not that you have a big problem with it anyway. But it's smart to, like, not do it. Either way, don't talk about it when they start filming. We have a morals clause. So even if you're giving up drugs . . . you know. They don't even want to know that you were on them in the first place."

"Yeah, I'm sure they won't use anything like that anyway," Lanny said, finding his voice. "When do they announce you guys, anyway?"

Chloe sounded a little choked up. "Soon, Lanny. Actually, it's embargoed . . ." she said the word in a business-like way because she'd just learned it, ". . . until next week. Then we do a whole bunch of TV interviews and magazine interviews to promote it."

"We're going to be bigger than when Michelle Trachtenberg did it," Simone said. "Trust me."

"That's because of our cool friendship, Simone," Chloe said bitterly. "In fact, I'm beginning to see that you might be my only *real* friend."

"Chloe—" I said, but she cut me off.

"Stop it, Nicole." Chloe stood up and looked around the table at us. "Seriously, you guys, I expected more support." We tried to backpedal, but you know how once a moment passes you can never get it back? Well, it had passed. "Simone, just tell them I'll be right back." She meant the camera crew, but she might as well have been talking about us. It felt like we'd just handed Chloe over to Simone.

Chloe stormed into the bathroom and didn't come out until the cameras were rolling, making it impossible for any of us to apologize or explain ourselves. All of us felt pretty bad for making an optimist like Chloe so upset, but we had our reasons for doubting she'd really sober up.

Simone just pretended like nothing ever happened and made sure the cameras caught her and Chloe being called into the kitchen to goof off with the chef in a bit that would later become famous for the chef's inability to peel his eyes off of Simone's cleavage.

Chloe and Simone looked like they were having a blast, and I think it's safe to say neither of them ever paid for their sushi again.

CHAPTER 10

Build Them Up

I KNEW FOR SURE that the Magdalena commercials
were going to be a big deal when I saw Chloe on TV while
I was working out. I stopped running in place and watched
in shock as she and Simone, arm in arm, sat on a lavender
sofa in Magdalena HQ being interviewed by Billy Bush.
Billy was doing the expected lovestruck banter with the
new BFFs as they giggled and flashed leg. Simone, inartic-
ulate to the point of mental incompetence, came off as
aloof and mysterious on TV for some unknown reason.
The camera loved Chloe, whose coke high read as girlish
excitement.

Their makeup? Perfection. Too *much* perfection, but
perfection.

"Chloe and Simone, how do you girls feel about being
the new Magdalenas?" Billy asked.

"It's cool," Simone said. "We're just being us. People can just, I don't know, hang out with us. Just by watching a commercial."

"How do you feel, Chloe?"

Without skipping a beat, she squeezed her own arm and laughed engagingly as she said, "I feel kind of soft." Of course Billy asked for a second opinion and reached over to squeeze her knee. Simone grabbed his hand and planted it on her own knee.

"See? Soft. That's what Magdalena's Beez Kneez Knee Moisturizer can do for you." If the cameraman wasn't careful, he was going to catch a lot more than Simone's knee—the girl was in a paisley Betsey Johnson, and I knew for a fact that she didn't own underwear. Chloe just kept smiling and playing along, but to me, it looked like Simone was not about to be eclipsed.

I didn't hear from Chloe that first week or so that the campaign was announced, which was ironic because I saw her everywhere on TV and her name popped up everywhere from the *L.A. Times* (snarky commentary on the latest superficial idiots Magdalena hoped to exploit) to the AOL homepage ("Meet Simone's BFF!"). The ads themselves would begin running in a month, an incredibly fast turnaround and yet par for the course with Magdalena, which spun the timing as proving their company was "of the moment" instead of proving how disorganized they were thanks to a CEO whose decrees could come down with about as much warning as Bambi had before her mother got shot.

When Chloe's number popped up on my cell at midnight one night, I was already in a car being driven home after the opening of a good friend's new boutique. I was nervous to answer it, wondering if she was going to pick up where she'd left off at Koi.

"Hi," I said softly. You can use your cell phone to communicate in so many ways other than by having a long conversation on it. People know you can see their number, so simply answering it already tells them, "I *want* to talk to you." If you answer it with "Hello?" as if you have no idea who might be calling, you're communicating distance. You're playing a game with them, and the game is going to end with them not getting whatever it is they're calling for. But saying "hi" like I did, acknowledging that I knew exactly who was calling and saying it with the gentleness of stroking a newborn kitten, was my way of apologizing and asking for another chance. Just . . . "hi."

"Hi," she said back, echoing my sentiments exactly. Nothing else had to be said about our blow-up for the moment.

"Clo, I've seen you all over TV. I'm so happy for you. This thing is gonna blow up."

"I know," she laughed. "I'm surprised. I thought it was a good opportunity, but I didn't know it could snowball. Imagine when they start airing the commercials. They've already filmed all this crazy stuff with us shopping, having lunch, hanging out with friends. Well . . . with Simone's friends."

I laughed at that. Maybe Chloe wasn't so out of it after all. Maybe she was going to be able to take what she needed, get out of the experience, and not let Simone's grandstanding detract from it.

"Nicole, I wanted to ask you a big favor," Chloe said in her little-girl voice. That voice took me back to what she'd been like in her childhood, when her love for being the center of attention had first surfaced.

Back then, there was a tambourine. These days, it sits in the corner of her old bedroom in her dad's Bel Air estate, tucked next to a tattered old Care Bear Grumpy I gave her when she got her tonsils out and a Teddy Ruxpin that broke when we tried to make it play Metallica. It would be gathering dust, except that a team of maids comes in to clean every other day, but the dark purple tambourine has long since faded to brown.

It had been custom made for Prince's 1984 *Purple Rain Tour*. Even though it was old and had lost a few of its bangles, Chloe probably could've sold it on eBay and bought one of those Fendi spy bags she was forever eyeing at Tracey Ross. But Chloe already *had* money, so she wasn't ever *about* money—instead, she'd probably give it to the Hard Rock in Vegas, so they could put it next to Mick Jagger's Chapstick.

But she wasn't done with it. That tambourine was a

symbol of her totally insane but completely fun childhood, and that alone made it the most valuable thing in the world to her. Chloe's first memory was of being on stage and playing that tambourine as the tiniest and least official member of the Revolution. She was three years old, and Prince liked to trot her out because, well, it didn't take a musical genius like Prince to see that Chloe belonged on stage. Her mom should have recognized Chloe's potential, too, and she would have if not for one problem—Chloe's biological mom was a Penny Lane–style groupie named Liv James.

Liv worshiped any guy with a guitar—and more than a few guys who stood guard backstage for guys with guitars or who broke down those stages for guys with guitars. When Chloe was born, despite (barely) having music in her genes, that wasn't enough to capture Liv's attention and interest. Motherhood was eleventh or twelfth on her Top 10 list of priorities, somewhere after getting into the Springsteen concert and before doing a load of laundry.

When Chloe was a baby, her mom would ask a friend to "babysit," and then leave for months on end to chase tours. Her life was just floating from place to place, like the feather in *Forrest Gump*. Even when she did take Chloe with her, Liv hardly ever noticed her.

Chloe's dad was even more of a nonfactor in Chloe's life. He wasn't even *with* the band—he was the *brother* of a member of the band. He carried Jolly Ranchers in his pocket and would sometimes give them to Chloe on the rare occasions he would run into her. Once, someone found a little blue pill definitely *not* for kids mixed in with the pile of candy and pocket lint he'd left for her.

For some people, it would have been the worst childhood ever, but Chloe made pink lemonade out of it. She may not have not gotten more than a few drops of attention from her mom, but she got gallons of it from just about every person she ever met. All she had to do was smile that ridiculously cute smile of hers, and they would be fawning all over her, no matter where she was.

While her mother put smiles on musicians' faces in dressing rooms, Chloe was bonding with the makeup people, who would cover her in glitter until every part of her sparkled—even the soles of her feet.

When Liv started running with some Prince hangers-on, Chloe captured the attention of the entire crew, even becoming the apple of Prince's eye—something Liv would have killed for, except even killing wouldn't have helped.

Prince had the tambourine made for Chloe and called her out on stage one night to hand it off to her.

"What's your name?" he asked, though he already knew it was Chloe James.

"Chloe," she said, instinctively shedding the part of her name that didn't matter so much. Then she played her little tambourine, working the crowd with her Shirley Temple showmanship as Prince excited them with *Darling Nikki*. The song went over her head, but the adoration didn't. Liv didn't have love to give, but she had inadvertently provided a magical substitute for it when she'd brought Chloe to the Prince show. It had led to Chloe staging her own elaborate mini-concerts, complete with her own lighting (lamps and nightlights) and stages (any sofa would do).

Unfortunately, all summer tours come to an end. And for Chloe, so did whatever flimsy bond she had with her birth mother—in Europe, Liv found a golden opportunity to end motherhood like it was a rained-out concert date and allowed Chloe to be adopted. Sad for Chloe at first, but by the time I met her not long after, she had already seemingly rebounded. There wasn't a trace of sadness about the newly rechristened Chloe Parker, who was now the daughter of two loving, attentive, successful, music-minded parents. She still had that teeny voice that had charmed Prince, and it always put a smile on my face—even when she was all grown up and putting it on for effect.

"Nicole, I wanted to ask you a big favor . . ."

I smiled, catching my own grin in the rearview mirror of my limo. "And what would that be?"

"Tomorrow we're doing this all-day photo shoot for Magdalena. It's *the* shoot. The only, like, *photo* shoot we're doing, and everything else is just video. It's probably the only time you'll ever see Mario Testino, Patrick Demarchelier, David Lachapeller, and Annie Leibovitz, in the same room at the same time. So once they do this, the pictures will be on billboards and in magazines and handed out everywhere." "And?"

Chloe went back to her grown-up voice. "I just wanted to know if you could come with me. I'd love to have you there."

"E-mail me the call sheet, and I'll see you then."

Wait, *who* was Chloe's best friend again?

CHAPTER 11

Take a *Picture . . .* It'll Last Longer

THE MAGDALENA PHOTO SHOOT started out as anything but picture perfect.

The shoot was held at AreA, an ultra expensive studio Downtown that had once been a massive warehouse for car parts. Now, it hosted body parts on a daily basis as all the top fashion photographers used it for half-naked models hawking, of all things, clothing. AreA was always an intimidating place to be, with its out-of-sight ceilings and fire-distressed walls. The rough look was not a pose—the place had been gutted by a devastating fire that had left it, well, even more perfect for the edgy uses to which it was put. Throw a painted model up against a wall that looks ready to disintegrate, and for whatever reason, it looks hot.

I got there late on purpose, to give Chloe a chance to

enjoy the attention on her own and so she could get started on hair and makeup. What I found was a very drugged-up girl sitting on a chrome barstool in a cavernous room surrounded by a bitchy posse of stylists and makeup people who all looked like they had stylists and makeup people of their own. Simone was already dressed (in Dress, naturally), coiffed, and doing solo shots against lavender seamless, giving good face to the photographer, a balding man with a ponytail and a beard shouting, "Effing great!" between clicks. The video crew was absorbed with Simone's every gesture, and someone was doing a quick interview with Simone's stylist Brittany, who was wearing Valentino mixed with Wal-Mart (a Jesse McCartney concert tee). Magdalena was seated in a director's chair with her usual entourage milling about, and Astrid was practically on bended knee in front of her. Why wasn't anyone noticing that Chloe was nowhere near ready?

I bee-lined to her, ignoring the hoopla and tuning out the techno music that blasted from everywhere and nowhere.

"What have you people done to her?" I demanded. Chloe barely registered that I was there.

"It's more like what she's done to *herself*," sniffed a tall, skinny, mixed-race, mixed-gender man with the requisite uniform of a makeup artist—Salvation Army cap, stolen CK jacket, Levi's jeans with a Dolce & Gabbana tag sewn on, and mismatched moccasins that somebody threw out.

"She's *messed up*," hissed the girl ratting Chloe's hair.

"She got here normal, went into the bathroom, and came out looking like Courtney Love."

"Listen," I said, looking over my shoulder to make sure no cameras were interested in our half of the room. "That's none of your business. Your business is to make her look amazing for this shoot. First of all, wash her hair. Towel dry it. Work some Dirt into it for texture, and let it fall naturally, side-parted—nothing structured." The chief hair girl nodded, accepting my alpha act.

I turned to the snippy stylist. "As for you, if it's already been decided that she's wearing anything but the clothes she walked in here with—whatever they are—then undecide it. These commercials are about their real selves, and if Chloe's got one thing going for her, it's her style. It's impeccable. Get her back into those clothes." He started to object, but I didn't let him. "If you just let her wear her own stuff, Magdalena will think you're a styling genius, and you'll get called over and over again. Here—" I snatched a gaudy epaulet right off his shoulder, where he'd pinned it that morning. "If you want to personalize the look and make your mark, you take this, and you string it up and let it hang off her neck—like a necklace. When you ink your licensing deal to mass market them, call me. Did everyone get that?"

The visibly chastened group of fashion guerrillas yessed me, and I excused us, grabbing Chloe off the stool. "We're going to the ladies' room for two seconds. When we come back, you'll take thirty minutes to fix her up. Then she'll shoot."

"Thank you, Nicole," Chloe moaned as I escorted her to the bathroom. "I don't know what happened; they just all started talking, and then Simone arrived already done. I didn't know she was going to do that—it just freaked me out so bad."

"That you used," I finished the thought for her. "I know. Believe me, I know."

"What is going oooooon?" Astrid popped her head up between us just before we hit the john. "People are saying she's high on drugs. She can't use drugs and be a Magdalena. Does she realize that? Do you realize that, Chloe? You do realize that? The morals clause all but *says* nobody can act a fool!"

I laughed gaily. "Astrid, you tell those jealous bitches to focus on their jobs. Chloe will be all ready in exactly thirty minutes and two seconds."

She calmed down a bit as Chloe forced a smile and batted her eyes at Astrid. If only she'd had that damn tambourine on her. But she didn't need it. Thankfully, Astrid bought what we were trying to sell.

"Okay," she said. "As long as it's not drugs. We're very *natural* at Magdalena."

I might be mistaken, but it looked like Magdalena herself might have been getting a little Botox on set as we all waited, but I didn't take the bait.

As soon as we were in the bomb-shelter bathroom, Chloe turned her face to me and looked me dead in the eyes. "I did a speedball. I know I'm messing up. I think I need help."

"Well, you've got me," I said. "And you've got Peggy and Julius."

"Yeah," she said, blinking away tears at the mention of her parents. "I hope I didn't mess things up with my parents."

Chloe had always adored her adopted parents, and their love affair with her had begun in the City of Love— Paris. Now, if I said the word "Paris" to Chloe, her head would flood with pictures of Chanel and The Ritz. But back when she was a kid, places didn't mean anything. Back then, all she ever saw were long cinderblock hallways in the backs of massive amphitheaters or bed-buggy hotel rooms where they would bring in a cot for her while her mother shared a king with whatever rocker she was rolling with that night.

Paris, France, could have been Cleveland, Ohio— except Julius and Peggy Parker were more likely to be found in Paris than in Cleveland.

Back then, in the world of pop music, Julius and Peggy Parker were like Prince Charles and Princess Diana, only without all the crazy drama. All of that would come later.

Julius was like a music magician, a producer/writer/all-around-genius who could pull number one hits out of his sleeves like rabbits with rhythm. He had the biggest smile ever created. The way Chloe described it, his smile looked like it started somewhere in the South, where he was born, and ended in Paris, where he had a chateau. He had this curly hair that from below with the light behind him— how little Chloe saw him—looked like a halo. To Chloe, Julius and Peggy *were* angels.

Julius radiated warmth like the sun, and Peggy, his high-school sweetheart and the true object of all those love songs that made women's hearts flutter, was like the wind: strong, beautiful, flowing, and full of energy. Peggy was one of the most transfixing figures little Chloe had ever seen.

Chloe's biological mom, Liv, never remembered any-one's name, and every time she walked into a restaurant, she insisted on the best table, all so she could sniff coke with the roadies and sleep with a drummer's brother. Julius had his weight in Grammies and insisted on carry-ing his own luggage, and Peggy was the kind of person who wrote thank-you notes to everyone, even the maids who ti-died her hotel rooms. Chloe's biological mom was full of herself, while Julius and Peggy were full of everyone *else*.

Julius and Peggy had been at one of Prince's Paris gigs, hoping to talk to some record people about installing Julius as a label head and to maybe get some tips from the man who was then the most popular live act in the world. Prince didn't let them get any of his treasured secrets, but they did pick up something better—a daughter.

Love at first sight is supposed to happen in date movies, but in Paris one night, it happened between a couple and a little girl. Julius and Peggy saw Chloe do some complicated dance moves to a little song she'd made up in her head, and they were hooked.

They took Chloe, her mom, and the whole backstage crew to some fancy place with chandeliers bigger than the flat she shared with Liv.

"Mommy, they're like upside-down castles!" Chloe observed. Julius later gave her those diamond chandelier earrings because they reminded him of that moment. Julius and Peggy were enchanted by her creative take, while Liv was under a table on the opposite end of the room.

As it got late, Peggy wrapped Chloe in her arms and told her stories in which Chloe was a princess in the most beautiful kingdom in the whole world while she made up songs. Chloe imagined her castle being made of crystal, like the chandeliers, and wanted all the rivers and streams to be made of strawberry soda. Chloe later told me she had never felt safer in her life than when she was in Peggy's arms, listening to her spin amazing fairy tales about Princess Chloe. She ended up having to spend the night with Julius and Peggy in their suite when Liv took off.

It would be a long while before Peggy would become Chloe's legal mother, but really, she became her mom that night.

The next day, Peggy and Julius took Chloe shopping and got her all new outfits, frilly and flowery things perfect for the tea parties and cotillions of their native South. It's funny now to think that this was Chloe's first real shopping trip. As she got older, shopping would become something that she would be doing about as often as most people stop for coffee. No one ever understood shopping was more than self-indulgence for Chloe—it was a memory of the first time she'd ever felt noticed and loved.

Peggy felt that Chloe was a special child whose gifts should be nurtured, something that wasn't going to happen as long as she stayed on as the unofficial backstage entertainment for Prince and his entourage, even if Chloe was having tons of fun and getting free Vanity dresses that fit the pre-schooler better than they fit Vanity. Peggy's maternal instinct told her that Chloe should stay with her. Even though Peggy didn't share DNA with this girl and Chloe didn't come from her womb, that night she'd slept in her arms, they'd shared a heartbeat and a bond that Peggy knew could blossom into something very special— maybe the most special thing in both of their lives.

Peggy campaigned hard to get Chloe invited back home to the States with them. At first, Julius wasn't sure— he was away on business all the time and too time-crunched for a family. Plus he knew something that Peggy didn't—that for various reasons, their marriage was not *quite* as strong as Peggy believed. Still, he'd agreed to it because there was something about the girl that just made him want to defy all logic. I guess you could call it love, which, if I've learned anything in life, has nothing to do with logic. He was also captivated by Chloe's uncanny ability to make up songs, as if God had meant for her to be the daughter of a musician—a daughter of Julius Parker's.

Liv was less of a challenge to convince than Julius had been. Chloe used to like to imagine that it was this big dramatic scene in Paris with moms fighting over her, or that later, when the proposed two-week visit turned into a month, a year, and then forever, Liv would cry or fight to keep her. But that just wasn't the case. If Liv had been given Sophie's choice, she would have been like, "Take 'em both."

Even through Chloe's recent ups and downs with drugs, which caused her to flounder in her creative aspirations, Julius and Peggy had never abandoned her, not even when they'd fallen out of love and abandoned each other. And I wasn't going anywhere either.

The same Bon Jovi song that DJ Ray had played in Chloe's honor at Mode was drifting in from the main studio as we exchanged a sisterly glance. It brought back visions of *Chloe: Unleashed*.

"Maybe I need to think about rehab," Chloe said.

I didn't say anything because I didn't have to. I was so proud of her.

The rest of the all-day photo shoot was pulled off without a hitch. The old drug-free Chloe was threatening to outshine the new drugged up one, and her mega-watt smile was flashing out Simone's own starry glow.

(And I'm still waiting for that phone call now that everyone is wearing epaulets as necklaces.)

CHAPTER *12*

The Mother of All
Confrontations

YOU KNOW WHAT'S really annoying? When you make up your mind to do something, then you waffle just a *tiny* bit, and then someone rides you to do it without knowing you're already on the case. It really steals your thunder. As she would relate to me in the longest text-messaging session ever recorded, Chloe had this problem after her Magdalena mega-shoot.

Chloe was mentally selling herself on the idea of rehab. "Nicole did it. Joey did it. It didn't work with him, but Joey did do it. It works for most people."

But as she headed east on Sunset and remembered that she was headed back home, to the house she shared with her mother, Peggy Parker, she started to feel all nervous and panicky. She needed to relax, and that was not something she could do on her own, at least not "pre-hab" as we now call it. So Chloe reached into the glove compartment while stopped at a light at Bundy and pulled out a Xanax, popped it in as the light changed, then washed it down with some Evian that had been sitting in the car *forever*. It wasn't a speedball, but she immediately knew it was cheating on her vow to give up drugs. Again.

"That's the last one," she said out loud to herself and meant it.

As she opened the front door of her house, the intercom clicked on.

"Chloe, come to my room, please."

Peggy Parker's low, serious voice echoed throughout the cavernous house. Chloe had heard these words so many times in her life, and it always meant the same thing—her mom had noticed something that Chloe had done that she thought was wrong and probably was, and now there was hell to pay.

The first time Chloe had heard that tone over that intercom was when she was twelve and had just gotten her second tattoo and her first body piercing. Finding someone who would ink you that young isn't hard, but it did mean driving out to the scary nether regions of the Valley and hanging in the garage of some biker dude named Tonsils. Peggy had been enraged at the tattoo, but Chloe later had it removed when she found out from her neighbor Cindy Hsu that the weak-looking Chinese symbol that was supposed to mean "flowering love" really meant "sleeping toad."

Chloe shuffled across the hardwood floor and pressed

the button on the kitchen intercom. "Give me a minute, Mom," she said, trying to raise her voice over the sound of Peggy's dogs barking loudly in the laundry room, where they were fenced in. "I'm gonna get some yogurt."

"Chloe, now please. And *shhhh*!"

The laundry room fell silent as the dogs immediately responded to Peggy's hushing. Likewise, Chloe had no choice but to respond to her mom's summons. She trudged up the back stairs, stopping off at her room to pick up her tambourine—she often worked it in her hands when she was having a difficult time as a reminder of the good old days. She noticed on her dresser her single remaining diamond chandelier earring and remembered how she'd lost one—lost one of the most precious things her father had ever given her—while she was messed up at Mode. Yet another reason rehab was a good idea. Then she marched toward the place that held as much fear and mystery for Chloe as any place on earth: her mother's room.

Some people's rooms are rooms—that's it. Other people's rooms are planets unto themselves. I'd been in her mother's room many times when Chloe and I were young and sneaky and let me tell you—Peggy Parker's bedroom fell into the second category. In some ways, Peggy's room was bigger than the entire house, or at least that's the way it seemed to us when we were little. The bed's pillows were the size of fallen trees and a billowing, gauzy canopy flowed to the hardwood floors, impossibly dark with islands of Persian rugs that Chloe imagined took a hundred people to make.

There were two closets filled floor to ceiling with an example of every idea ever had by every designer who ever worked a sewing machine since Julius had his first hit record.

She had her own kitchen in there behind French doors, and the largest bathroom in any private residence on the West Coast. The entire wall on the western side of the room was made up of windows. Open, they seemed like they held the entire sky. Mostly, though, this effect was lost because the windows could be blotted out by remote control, and that's how Peggy Parker liked it. To Chloe, it seemed that her mother was turning on and off the sun when she pushed the button. More than a decade after her divorce, Peggy Parker still liked the sun turned off more often than she liked it turned on.

As Chloe made her way into her mother's room, it was like Peggy was already talking to her. She was *that* on it.

". . . and Chloe, my dear, my sweet," said Peggy, sitting on the couch, ready for bed in white silk pajamas and a floral kimono, "what in the hell are these?"

Peggy held two silver spoons from her kitchen between her fingers like chopsticks, the backs facing Chloe. They had ugly black splotches—burns. Chloe knew what the hell they were because she'd burned them. She was getting caught doing the last speedballs of her life.

Rather than answer, Chloe proceeded to take her position—which is what she always did when her loving mother turned into a dragon lady over a mistake Chloe had made. Chloe headed into the bathroom and climbed into the empty jacuzzi, the place she liked to be when her mom was yanking her head off and during other seismic tremors. She fondled a Lalique swan and inhaled the scented candles, which smelled better than the exotic fruits whose natural aromas they were designed to emulate.

"Not only do we know you did this Chloe, but we know why," Peggy said, following her in. She always said "we" even though she only meant herself. "You are showing total disregard for the things in this house, young lady, a total disrespect for decency and for your own body and for your time on this earth. Who taught you to do this? To trip the lizard?"

Chloe laughed before she could stop herself. "It's chasing the dragon, Mom." But the question was just as hilarious. Who had taught Chloe about drugs? Peggy asked it like she might have seen it on an episode of *Law & Order* or something. The answer could have been that Chloe grew up around famous musicians who were friends of the Parkers and who constituted a veritable Syringes Across America. More accurately, the problem could be traced—as so many problems could be—back to Simone.

Peggy and Julius Parker's marriage was falling apart around the time that Simone was first teaching Chloe about drugs, sex, and other things no tween needed to hear about from the likes of her. Their divorce was a gradual, if not exactly quiet, thing. Thanks to the great invention known as the intercom, Julius and Peggy Parker didn't actually need to be in the same room to rip each other to shreds, and voices carried in big Hollywood mansions. Peggy always knew Julius was probably cheating on her when he was on the road—she just preferred not to see it. But when Julius made not seeing it impossible—panties left on purpose in his luggage, a woman's laughter in the background when Peggy would call Julius in his hotel room—Peggy would start in on the intercom, screaming her displeasure and the Parker's entire staff heard.

The tabloids would write about her parents' divorce like it was a boxing match—and sometimes it was. Once, Chloe watched in horror as Julius attempted to zoom off in his Maserati to wherever it was he went when he fought with Peggy, except Peggy wasn't letting him go. She stood in front of the car, her hands on the candy-apple red hood. There was no keeping Julius from avoiding her rage, so the car lurched forward. Peggy rolled up the hood like it was the long tongue of some crazy monster trying to swallow her whole. Julius kept going, the back tires squealing and spitting out gravel from the driveway, his soon to be ex-wife holding on to his car for dear life.

The bright side of this episode was that neither Peggy nor Julius had ever had to sit Chloe down to tell her they were divorcing. The dark side was that Chloe and Simone were spending a lot of unsupervised time together as The War of the Parkers dragged on. With Peggy on her own planet (in her room) and Julius off doing his thing, part of Chloe's adolescence became a giant sleepover at Simone's, where they would freak themselves out watching *The Si-*

lence of the Lambs on the VCR or work themselves into a lather watching *Beverly Hills 90210* on TV. Even then Simone was bad news, wondering aloud how large Steve Sanders's cock was. She was already stealing lingerie from her mom's stash and sharing it with Chloe, teaching her innocent friend how to hold and inhale a joint and snorting leftover coke. The Drew Barrymore crash course in how to be a teen junkie might have gotten even worse if it wasn't for an unauthorized field trip that broke up the girl gang of two for the next several years.

It was Simone's uncle Tim Westlake's idea to take Terence and the girls to Vegas to show them the new Excalibur, where he had a comped suite. No one thought to tell Peggy and Julius about the trip, and none of the Westlakes noticed when the girls took their driver to the Beverly Center on the way to the airport for "supplies" that could only be found at Contempo and Judy's. Along with lip gloss, eye glitter, high heels, and thigh highs, Chloe and Simone picked up these cheap elastic-and-velvet bell-bottom pantsuits that had bell-sleeve blouses, Simone's red and Chloe's green. They promptly threw the pants in the mall trashcan on the way to the car—being eleven-going-on-twelve, they were short enough that they only needed the tops.

When they got to Vegas, the girls didn't spend much time at the cheesy Excalibur. Poolside, Simone had met some older boys who were staying at the Mirage, which was way cooler than the Excalibur, and she'd gotten them to invite her and Chloe over to their hotel to listen to music and watch cable. So the girls packed their velvet shirts-cum-micromini dresses and all their makeup in Chloe's *Mickey Mouse Club* backpack, told Terence that they were going to Circus Circus, and changed in the back of a cab. They were sure to slather the makeup on real thick because they knew this would be their only chance to use it.

Hanging out with the boys was innocent enough even after they'd changed into the garish outfits—though two eleven year olds dressed like streetwalkers and hanging out with a bunch of beer-swilling tenth graders in baseball caps and football jerseys wasn't exactly wholesome. Chloe and Simone had sipped some Budweiser beers and danced even though someone insisted on playing Garth Brooks (*ew!*) before the boys ditched them to go test out their fake IDs at a strip club, where adult women with actual breasts and stuff might be. Chloe and Simone wound up wandering around downtown Vegas in their microminis and heels at 9:30 P.M. asking tourist dads on Freemont for directions.

When the police let Peggy and Julius know their daughter was in Las Vegas and had been picked up as a suspected child prostitute, the Parkers and the Westlakes had, to put it mildly, stopped socializing, and Peggy had forbidden Chloe from *ever* going next door to the Westlake house again. Chloe was cooped up at home for a while, but Simone had no such restriction—she was always allowed to come and go as she pleased.

A couple of years later, when Peggy and Julius had forgotten how poisonous their daughter's friendship with Si-mone could be and Chloe was invited to hang with Si-mone one summer weekend, she discovered Simone had gone from a bad influence to worse.

The Westlake house was unchanged—that family had a weird thing for drapes with patterns of naked Greek sculptures, real rip-off Versace stuff that belonged in a gay guy's South Beach condo, but Simone was different. She was like Simone on speed—well, actually, she *was* Simone on speed. She was stuffing her bra with expensive silk scarves "that, like, people make from really rare moths, so they feel like human skin" and warning Chloe never to use toilet paper for fear "your tits will smell like ass, and no guys will ever want to sleep with you."

If you aspired to be a drug addict, Simone was a good friend to have. She loved drugs and spending money. A plain black Narcisco Rodriguez to wear only once for a mere $295? Why not? Meg Ryan had one, and Simone was way cuter, which was how Simone explained it to Chloe. Overspending on clothes meant that neither the Westlakes nor the Parkers would notice if there was an extra $400 or $500 missing after a shopping trip. Simone mostly liked coke, pills, and pot (she had a strain of weed named after her by age sixteen). Chloe mostly liked heroin (thanks to a quasi-Romeo-and-Juliet-without-the-Romeo relationship with Joey later on), coke, pills, and E.

It was glamour, parties, and friendship—in that order—just like this season's Magdalena tagline.

Chloe hadn't hit skid row until now, years later, because the influential Simone had finally been shipped off to a superharsh boarding school for the pathologically wayward, and the Westlakes had then moved back to South Africa, returning a year or so before Magdalena caught wind of the hardly reformed Simone and her potent ability to make young girls do things they shouldn't—in her personal life, take drugs; in TV ads, in theory, buy overpriced makeup.

"Mom," Chloe said through laughter and tears from the jacuzzi. "Mom, I won't be chasing any dragons again, and I'm sorry I wrecked your spoons." She tapped her sad little tambourine. It was faded and unpretty, but it still made music.

"Baby," Peggy said firmly, "it's not my spoons that I'm worried about. And it's not the spoons I'm mad as hell at."

Chloe looked back over her shoulder at her serious-as-cancer mother. "Mom, I'm being real with you here—I have a big problem. It's a problem I've had ever since . . . well, for a long time. Off and on. Lately, it's been on." Peggy tried to interrupt with another loud sermon, but Chloe wouldn't cede her the floor just yet. "Mother! Mom, let me finish what I started. Look, what I'm trying to tell you is that a few days ago I swore off drugs. I don't want to screw up my big chance with Magdalena because I *know*—I know on my own—that there's not enough concealer in the world to hide being a skanky drug addict. Which I'm not. But I made that vow, and then I backtracked a little with the . . . spoons . . . and maybe with some Xanax. I already talked with Nicole about this, and I'm trying to figure out the best way to get into a *place* somewhere to get some help on my vow—without interfering with the Magdalena deal."

Neither of them said anything for a long time, and Peggy didn't say anything at all. She never responded to her daughter's remarkable speech. Instead, Chloe just gradually became aware of the brilliant colors on the sleeves of her mother's kimono as her arms encircled Chloe from behind. Peggy hugged her tightly around the neck, kissing Chloe on the head just like she used to when Chloe was that size standing up, back when she was a psychedelic Shirley Temple and still made up songs for no reason at all.

CHAPTER 13

The Heroine Takes a Fall

THE NEXT DAY I picked up Clo, and we drove to Mikela's place in Malibu. She lived in her dad's Moroccan mansion, a temple of group sex, primo drugs, and impeccable rock-n-roll in the 1960s—and not much had changed since then. Even drug free, I always found it so peaceful up there with all the bamboo, and eucalyptus, and this giant fig tree that could've been older than the whole city.

Mikela greeted us at the sixteen-foot carved-wood door with one of her trademark naked hugs.

Sipping 7Up and eating ham sandwiches brought out by a smiling maid, we laid out by the pool under the broiling sun, protected by sun block ninety-nine, and talked about the Magdalena build-up. The latest thing to hit was a partial cover of *Life & Style* of Simone walking hand in hand with Jack Osbourne. To me, it was such an obvious attempt to hijack some of Jack's "jeez, you got skinny" press. Chloe wasn't quite sold yet on my the-devil-is-a-woman-and-her-name-is-Simone platform, so I didn't push it. She and Mikela oohed and ahhed over the magazine despite knowing some of the people in it personally.

"You know what I don't get?" Mikela said, brushing the crumbs off her bare chest. "Simone and I have been, like, sleeping together for two years, and nobody's ever even written about it. I mean, not even *Star*. What's that all about?"

We didn't really have a good answer as we each flipped back through our brains for the millions of hints we'd ignored.

"I had to kiss a girl in my first movie," I said. "I should have called you to run lines with me, Mikela."

Talk eventually turned to the real reason for our visit—we wanted to tell Mikela about Chloe's renewed resolve to kick drugs and discuss her rehab options with an expert—we both knew her family was connected to a rehab facility that might be right for Chloe's needs.

"Honey, I'm so proud of you," Mikela said, lighting a joint. We looked at her in disbelief. "What? Oh, sorry—the E I took was too chemical-ly." She scrunched her face up as she said it, then ignored the poor timing of her puffing. "Anyway, rehab is so much fun. My dad was on the board of directors of one in the desert where you go camping and ride horses. We can totally get you in. You're going to love it. All the boys in rehab are totally available because their girlfriends have all given up on them. It's fantastic."

"Is it outpatient?" Chloe asked. "I need to come and go—I have the commercials to do, and they don't exactly want to film me in rehab."

"For sure," Mikela said, "not a problem."

"Miss Mikela?" the maid startled me by sneaking up behind us while we were talking. I felt like a kid caught doing something bad. "Your friends are here." Chloe and I covered up as Joey sauntered in with Natasha. Mikela didn't bother, instead standing up and kissing them both. Natasha wasn't used to Mikela's raw lifestyle and wore her discomfort in the form of a scowl that looked like a head wound. Chloe, predictably, got a little antsy with Joey and his new squeeze around. She cell phoned Chip and started telling him about how she was going to rehab and he'd have to support her. I'd almost forgotten about Chip. She didn't know it yet, but so had Chloe.

"Well, kids, I'm off," I said, grabbing my stuff. "I need to get to the studio." I asked Chloe if she was coming or if she could get home later, and she waved me off and hugged me good-bye.

Maybe I should have known better than to leave her alone, but you can't be with someone all the time.

As I later pieced together from frantic phone calls and some eyewitness accounts in the bad press that followed like a gaseous cloud after a chemical explosion, the afternoon did not end the way anyone expected after I departed.

Joey had motored after dropping Natasha at Mikela's, then called later to ask her to make a pickup of some pick-me-up for him on her way home. Trouble was she had no wheels, and Mikela never learned to drive. Mikela barely knew Natasha and had muttered something about what driver's ed classes must be like in Siberia, so she wasn't wild about loaning out her mom's car to her. That left Chloe, a girl on the verge of rehab, as designated driver of Mikela's dad's Caddy on a drug run for two eightballs of cocaine. Why did she agree to do it? More than half the reason was probably her pesky pining for Joey. Chip had taken his place but hadn't filled his shoes. DJ Ray had possibilities, but he wasn't yet completely in the mix.

But Chloe also later confessed to a strange line of reasoning so warped it had the ring of authenticity: She'd actually been excited by the idea of being *around* drugs without *using* them. It was some kind of personal test.

Here's a tip: if you ever see a girl like Chloe or one of her friends either south of Olympic or east of Highland, it's a pretty safe bet that they're running an illegal errand.

You get the impression that drug dealers are these skeezy Black Panther types, but there are as many different kinds of drug dealers as there are drug users and drugs. This particular drug dealer was a middle-aged Mexican woman in a housedress who didn't speak English and lived with her family in an old Gothic house on the top of a hill somewhere around Pico and Robertson.

When Chloe and Natasha got there, it was what Chloe's dad always referred to as earthquake weather—cold, dark, and overcast for no reason after being really, really hot. No earthquake was coming, but something pretty close to it was on the way.

A fourteen-year-old boy who introduced himself as Junior and served as their translator met Natasha and Chloe at the door. On the floor was a girl who looked like she was four and a little baby in a bouncy chair who was laughing at her sister. Chloe wasn't sure if she should wave to them or look away. She looked away. The TV blasted soccer in Spanish as Junior asked them in perfect, unaccented English, "Would you like a sample of the product?"

Chloe and Natasha would have been really freaked out if they ever bothered thinking about it. I mean, the girl on the floor was like the same age that Chloe was when she met Julius and Peggy. How twisted is that? How twisted was it that this was a place Joey apparently came to on a regular basis? How twisted was it that he was now sending his current girlfriend and his ex-girlfriend there unescorted? Chloe would later realize this was the moment when she stopped crushing on Joey.

Natasha took a sample from one of the bags neatly ordered on the Formica table in the living room. Chloe, to her utter astonishment, passed. The lady was cooking arroz con pollo in a big black pot, and she only left the stove to take their money, count it, and stick it in the pocket of her apron.

Outside, Chloe and Natasha exchanged looks over the roof of the car, Chloe unlocked the doors, and they got in.

All Chloe could remember of the accident was starting the car and pulling out before trying to put it into gear— but for some reason not being able to.

Natasha recalled cursing like a demon and moving the gearshift up and down. "There's something wrong with the gears!" she shouted as the Cadillac rolled backward down the hill, gaining speed as it headed toward Robertson. Chloe was frozen, but Natasha managed to steer the car in reverse which, I mean, kudos to the driver's-ed classes of Mother Russia after all. Their short, dangerous trip ended when the Caddy ran a red light and crumpled up into a fire hydrant, narrowly missing some pedestrians who were crossing.

Natasha called her parents, and when they asked the obvious question, "What the hell were you doing at Pico and Robertson?" she made some truly lame excuse about knowing a guy who took really good headshots.

Meanwhile, both girls were having unflattering head-shots made without their knowledge—it turned out a pa-parazzo had been following them the entire time, and since neither of them were famous (even Chloe was only on the way), they weren't used to making sure they weren't being tailed every ten seconds like I am.

All Chloe's mind could think, over and over, was, "You can't get arrested. You can't get arrested. And you can't go to the hospital because you have drugs on you." See, because Chloe had already *been* arrested. Twice. Both times when she was past eighteen. If she got strike three, she was likely to do something she'd never dreamed of: jail time.

The first time had been when she went to this fabulous agent's party where there were more flowers than Chloe had ever seen before. The place smelled better than any perfume. She wanted her whole world to smell like it did when you walked into that party.

These really tall women in really long silver gowns handed everyone flutes of Kristal as they entered, including illegals like Chloe. Peggy drank several and spent the rest of the night talking to this really cute musician. She barely noticed when Chloe stole two sips of champagne.

But it was only two sips. And that's what Clo told the cop who pulled her over after she California-rolled through a stop sign a block from her house with a sloshed Peggy in the passenger seat.

"At least *she* wasn't driving," Chloe said to the cop, gesturing to her mom, and they shared a laugh. Cops *loved* Chloe.

He asked for her driver's license, which almost by chance she actually had and told her to get out of the car.

She blew her two sips of champagne right into the Breathalyzer. The cop agreed that she was okay to drive. And then he arrested her. When you're underage, it doesn't matter whether or not you're impaired: If you blow anything into the Breathalyzer, you're busted.

But still Chloe had this idea that she didn't break the law, even though she did, and she was arrested for it. She didn't take her arrest seriously until she was arrested again.

Fast forward to a little over a year later and jump across the country to New York City. When she left, Chloe was wearing a Missoni bikini, a white transparent dress, and no shoes, which amounted to every piece of clothing she had taken with her on her surprise trip to the Big Apple with Simone.

Chloe's mother started yelling at her while she was nodding off by the pool, telling her she was wasting her life and squandering her musical talent by drinking herself into a stupor, so Chloe had simply run out without changing. While tearing down the hill in her car, she called Simone, who was at the Santa Monica Airport just getting on the Westlake family plane. Simone told her that if she could get there in fifteen minutes, she could come with her to Manhattan. Fourteen minutes later, Chloe stepped onto the plane, barely dressed.

Chloe spent her first day in New York doing drugs and lounging at the Plaza, the second day pillaging Peggy's open account at Saks, and the third day inciting a riot. Simone and a bunch of her friends took Chloe along to a superswanky club in SoHo everyone was talking about called Exit 10.

Even though at that point Chloe had bought like a September issue of *Vogue*'s worth of clothing at Saks, for some reason she was still wearing the same outfit she flew over in: Missoni bikini and see-through sundress. Call it drug-addict couture.

There were lots of trendies at the club and lots of drama. Simone's friend Jolie, a model, was dating this guy Daedalus, who was the black sheep son of a senator or congressman or something, only their dating looked like most people's break-ups. At the crowded club, which was *so hot* even though Chloe was pretty much wearing nothing, Daedalus poured an entire bottle of Ketel One on Jolie's head, and it all waterfalled onto Chloe. The vodka felt frightening on her skin, like it was going to freeze all of it off and then burn her flesh. She was pissed that she hadn't even been drinking that night—only pills!—and now she was stinking like an alkie. And even though she'd just met Jolie, she was Simone's friend (not hers), and that guy was a total dick for doing this to her.

Five minutes later, after things died down, Chloe had grabbed a carafe of cranberry juice and flung it at the guy, triggering a massive bar fight that Chloe managed to slip out of, into a cab, and up to Simone's suite at the Plaza to chill out and take some more Xanax. Flinging cranberry juice over a completely worthless jerk must be a federal offense because two days later the police were calling Chloe on her cell, telling her that she needed to meet them and that she should get a lawyer. Daedalus was telling them that Chloe had stabbed him in the eye with glass, in hopes that she would maim or kill him, or something very Hannibal Lechter like that.

They called it felony assault with a deadly weapon, which sounds much worse than attack with a tart-but-sweet refreshment. Julius and his lawyers helped get Chloe off with probation despite her having to plead no contest. He'd been the only popstar of all time with no drug problem, so it shocked him when Peggy informed Julius that their daughter's troubles might be somehow linked to substances other than cranberry juice.

"Oh, Chloe," he'd said, quiet in the way that Peggy was always loud. "This is on your permanent record. This isn't like getting thrown out of school. You have been arrested, and that is going to follow you."

Chloe debated whether or not that was a good point to mention to Julius that this was actually her second arrest.

And now, with Mikela's mom's car and a fire hydrant the only casualties thank God, Chloe was staring down the barrel of a possible third arrest. Chloe Parker, ballerina, straight-A student, secret drug addict trying to turn her life around, could do hard time if she couldn't get out of there.

At that moment, Lanny arrived on the scene in his T-bird like Superman saving the day. He'd been over to Mikela's and didn't like the sound of an all-girl drug run. How right he'd been. He stepped out of his car just as gawkers were beginning to surround the Caddy.

"People, I'm a resident down the street at Cedar's," he said, trying to sound doctorly as he approached the vehicle. Natasha was hyperventilating in Russian, and Chloe was staring straight ahead in shock.

"Natasha! Are you guys hurt at all? What happened?"

She took a deep breath and told him in as few words as possible what was done and what needed to be undone. "We made a pickup. The gear stuck. We need to get out of here."

"All right, everyone, step back, please," Lanny said, sitting halfway on Chloe's lap and starting the car up again. It was running. The gear wasn't stuck; it was locked with some kind of anti-theft device Mikela's parents had installed. It couldn't have been on earlier, but somehow it had clicked on while they were in el drug den. Gadget Boy disabled it and helped shovel Chloe into the backseat, so Natasha could drive.

"Okay, Natasha—drive to Joey's and don't run any red lights. I'll meet you there."

With that, the perps tore off, and Lanny got back into his ride, also leaving the scene. If it weren't for the unauthorized headshots, no one might have known what happened that day. But when you're famous—or even on your way to being famous—one of the side effects is loss of privacy, and that includes the anonymity required to actually get away with stuff.

The following day, Chloe called me to tell me everything about an hour before the first pictures of the scene showed up on Stawker.com. They would later run in their entirety in *Bitz* and every other tabloid, leading the till then clueless cops straight to Chloe's door. Chloe felt lucky that Peggy didn't murder her in a crime of passion when the police arrived, but she believed her when she told her it had not been a drug-related accident (not in the way people were insinuating, anyway).

Unfortunately, while the accident only had minor legal ramifications—some fines, some warnings, some suspended licenses—the ensuing fall-out definitely gave Magdalena, both the company and the woman, pause. Magdalena was about to invest millions in an ad blitz that involved two beautiful socialites, and one of them apparently did her socializing in drug dens before rolling down hills and into photogenic accidents. The morals clause was undoubtedly being studied very closely. You could tell because when asked to comment on the mysterious accident, Astrid's corporate press release left the door wide open, "We have no comment one way or another at this time."

Chloe was really sweating it out when she was summoned, along with Simone, to Magdalena HQ. She arrived alone—I wasn't needed to hand-hold anymore—and steeled herself for the possibility that she was going to lose her contract.

Magdalena was seated at the head of the conference table, fuming to the point where the air around her looked kinda wavy. The camera crew was taping everything, much to Chloe's surprise. Simone was giving the cold shoulder, but then her shoulder was never truly warm.

"I'm not sure this is the best idea," Magdalena said to Astrid, gesturing to the cameras. Astrid nodded confidently. She was a piece of work, that Astrid, but she knew what she was doing. "At any rate—Chloe."

"Yes, Magdalena?" Chloe felt a little funny and was trying to put her finger on it—oh, yeah, she wasn't wasted.

"Chloe, we're all very upset about your accident. We're ever so glad you're *okay*, but we're ever so concerned that this accident may have been the tip of the iceberg and that Magdalena is the *Titanic*. We can't have girls representing us involved with drugs." She said the word "drugs" like someone in a 1950s PSA bad-mouthing reefer.

"I don't have the problem," Simone clarified helpfully. "Drugs are not cool."

Chloe took a deep breath. "I don't have a problem either, Magdalena. At least, what I'm trying to say is that the accident didn't happen because I was high—that much is true. But I do think it's important for me to be real with you and tell you that I *have* had some substance-abuse problems."

Simone feigned shock. Astrid didn't have to feign it— she *was* shocked. She'd thought Chloe would deny any drug use to the hilt and that it would make for great, family-friendly TV. Astrid wanted some drugs of her own right then.

"Is that so?" Magdalena asked, her voice losing some of that unplaceable accent it always seemed to have. It sure wasn't a Bronx accent, though that's where her birth certificate said she'd been born a few years before Elizabeth Taylor and a few after Prohibition.

"Yes," Chloe said. "But I'm telling you this because even before this accident, I had decided that while I'm not a basket case or anything, I'm going to be entering re-hab. I've already signed up with the help of my friend Mikela, whose family's car I accidentally wrecked. Oopsy."

Magdalena semi-smiled at this, and the camera ate it up like a shark does chum.

"Go on."

"No amount of makeup can cover up your inner prob-lems, so I'm going to address those and let the makeup handle the minor flaws."

Silence.

Then, sensing the tide turning, Simone embraced Chloe. This was the first person she'd full-on hugged who wasn't nude and thrusting in her whole life. "Oh, Clo," she sobbed, "I'm always here for you, girlfriend. I'm al-ways, like, here for you."

"And . . . scene," Astrid whispered. It was definitely a perfect mini-drama, one that when cut into a sixty-second spot would truly speak to America's spotty youth. Who needed makeup more than well-off heroin addicts con-templating kicking their habits, anyway?

"And we un-der-*stand*," Magdalena said, her voice ris-ing with each syllable back to its usual thunderous, femi-nine roar, "and we *forgive* you. And we will let you stay on as a Magdalena. You and Simone both."

Chloe had gotten her ass into trouble, and now she had gotten her own ass out of it.

That was progress.

CHAPTER *14*

Back to Where She Started

T HE NEXT STEP after getting one's ass out of trouble is getting one's ass into rehab, which Chloe did the following morning packing up all of her Juicy sweat suits and Havaianas flip-flops, after hugging us all good-bye following a festive buh-bye brunch at The Ivy. Chloe looked radiant—it was unfortunate that Magdalena didn't shoot the brunch, but Astrid had convinced Magdalena to quit while they were ahead. They'd start to parcel out the world's first reality commercials (isn't that an oxymoron?) the day after Chloe made a triumphant exit from twenty-eight days in rehab. Magdalena had decided she wanted rehab to work for her golden goose, so she insisted that Chloe go and stay—no checking in and out.

"This is not summer school," Magdalena told Chloe passionately. "This is the school of hard knocks!" She'd known Billie Holliday personally, so she knew whereof she spoke.

Chloe would have both company in and a free ride to rehab in the form of none other than a remorseful Joey. When he'd realized the frightening situation into which he'd so glibly put two girls he cared about, he finally figured out for himself that Joey the Junkie as a nickname was not going to work for him. He asked Chloe for forgiveness, and she gave it easily. Both Natasha and I—for different reasons—were not comfortable with the idea that Joey and Chloe would be handcuffed together in an upscale rehab facility with plenty of opportunities to fall back in love, but in the same way that Chloe's drug vow had impressed me, so did her conviction about Joey.

"I'm over him, Nicole—completely. I love him as a friend. But I don't love him." Kicking drugs was going to be easy if she could kick Joey's charisma.

Chloe wrote me long letters—actual *letters*, no texting or calling—from the desert. She said she felt like Florence of Arabia out there, roughing it. Well, they had plasma TVs in their rooms, drank specially blended teas, and ate exquisite yogurts with real fruit blended into them, so "roughing it" wasn't quite the right phrase. But I cut the girl some slack since she was making such a big self-improvement.

The media ate the whole thing up, at first focusing on Chloe's brave decision, then on Simone's loyal support from outside, then on Simone falling off a motorcycle while zooming around on a friend's estate (the Magdalena cameras magically caught this one, hmmm), then on Simone rescuing a woman who almost stepped out in front of a speeding car. Notice a trend here? Simone had perfected the art of self-absorption as a baby. As a grown woman, she was perfecting the art of self-projection.

What can I say about the reality of drug rehab? Kicking heroin is kind of like the worst flu you ever had combined with the worst food poisoning you could imagine, and then times the whole thing by about forty. This sounds pretty bad, and actually it's much worse than that, but the point is that it *ends*—the physical part, at least—the mental part takes longer. Plus they have some entirely unpleasant drug to make the whole nasty-ass physical part go quicker.

Xanax is different—less vomiting, more surprise freak-outs. The Xanax detox takes a long three weeks, and instead of being like heroin detox—a steady and consistent mix of no sleep and barfing—you never know what to expect coming down off Xanax.

Chloe was on seizure medication for the whole stretch and on suicide watch for the first ten days because people withdrawing from Xanax don't know what to do with all the pain during those first few weeks, and the only way they can think of handling it is suicide. Fortunately, Chloe's Xanax addiction was not as severe as they come, so she never came close to ending it all.

The facility had a nurse go everywhere with her—while she peed, and showered, and looked at the photo books that were lying around the place, she had a shadow.

There were two nurses assigned to her, one by day and one by night. Chloe hated it for twenty-four hours and then started to really like it—it was like having guardian angels, albeit guardian angels keenly interested in how to get Magdalena discounts.

I never visited Chloe because she asked me not to. But she did have visitors. Halfway through rehab, I got this letter, which was dated "the fourteenth day of the rest of my life."

N:

Maybe they call it rock bottom because so many rock stars end up here? Rumor was that Eminem was here, then that turned into Kevin Federline, then we all figured out the guy was nobody famous. Who knew they had gossip in rehab? Depressingly, I'm the most famous person in here. Or is that totally cool?

You were right—they do have you make long lists of people you need to forgive and the different categories of the types of things you need forgiveness for. Then you have to write a story or essay about it, and finally you have to draw pictures of how you perceive your parents and yourself. It was very sixth-grade science fair . . . remember? When we drew the planets?

My mom and dad came for the drawing part,

which was group therapy. Imagine them in the same room together! People weren't allowed to ask my dad for autographs, but he gave some out on the sly. He said my drawing of him was "ridiculous." It was basically a toothy smile with wavy hair. He was wearing pajamas with stars all over them and had each of his feet on two separate islands. One was called "Not Here," and the other was called "Someplace Else."

In my picture of Mom, I showed her behind bars—it was supposed to be the intercom. Half of her was asleep and smiling, and the other half was awake and screaming, her hair reduced to being six snakes.

She said, "Medusa???!!!" and asked if I thought she could turn me to stone. I swear she almost did right then. She got from the picture that if she was awake, she was yelling. All the parents were freaking out over their own kids' drawings.

"We wouldn't be so far away if you weren't pushing us," my dad said.

When I told him there was nothing there to push—they both got it.

My dad ended up apologizing for not "stopping the fire until the whole plantation was filled with smoke." I forgave him, and he forgave me. Then Mom said she was sorry for not finding better ways to communicate. Picturing her not yelling at me is like picturing Flava Flav without that big clock around his neck, so it felt like a really big deal, Nicole. I forgave her, and she forgave me.

Rehab is way heavy. But I think it's working.

Never guess who else came to see me! (No, not her.) The nurse lady told me a gentleman was waiting for me. I thought she just meant Joey. Sidebar: Joey's doing good . . . lots of puking, tho. But he's playing this grand piano they have here and writing new music for me to sing to.

But when I went out to the waiting room thinking it would be Joey wanting to hit the piano with me, there was DJ RAY. I'm so not kidding right now. Ray drove all the way out here to the middle of the desert with some flowers for me and a mix CD. The flowers smell great, the CD sounds great, and Ray hugs great. I know! I don't know what to think. But we'll have to give this some careful thought when I'm sprung.

Carrie and Lanny sent me a joint letter, by which I mean they both sent it, not that there was a joint in it, which was nice. No word from Mikela, but she got me in here, and oh, there is a giant nude painting of her in the lobby, so I feel she's with me in spirit. Let's just say Chip hasn't even called. W/E!

I hope the press is being kind to me out there (?), and Simone isn't too mad (???), and I still have a job like I think I do—the plasmas here only show closed-circuit movies. I've seen *Spice World* so many times I want to use again. JUST KIDDING.

Bye,

Sober Spice

P.S. I'm glad that I made you promise not to come because you are *too busy* and because you are my lifeline to the real world. I'll be that much happier to see you when I get out!

Chloe's departure from rehab had everything but a red carpet, including Mary Hart waiting to quiz her on changing her lifestyle and what kind of lifestyle she was now hoping to sell kids with her Magdalena campaign.

When she first walked out the door a few feet behind a shockingly all-American-looking Joey, I didn't recognize my old friend. Chloe always had that trendy heroin-chic frame—you know, ribs, boobs, sunken cheeks, and fat, juicy lips. But if she'd been vomiting the first couple of weeks while kicking horse, she'd more than made up for it with the last two weeks' feasting. Apparently, rehab had a bitchin' chef because Chloe had put on a solid fifteen.

"She's back, and she's got back!" Mary told the cameras.

Chip, who hadn't been on the scene since, uh, decking her, was there, too. He smiled and said "yeah" when asked by media if he was Chloe's man. Then he handed out copies of his band's demo.

Simone was in hot pink and was all over Chloe in a hot minute, hugging her, praising her for completing rehab, and clearly—to me, at least—gloating over the bloating. "Clo, we're friends to the end. No matter what. 'Kay?" The Magdalena cameras caught every scripted word, zooming in for Chloe's response.

"Kay." Edit. "Where's Nicole and the gang?"

Chloe spotted her real best friends and ran over to us, bear-hugging me, then Mikela, then Carrie (who we considered leaving behind when we took off), and finally Lanny, the knight in shining armor who'd turned her potential drug bust into at worst a mildly embarrassing traffic incident and at best a career peak.

"Chloe!" Lanny exclaimed, looking her up and down. "You look . . . amazing! You're so curvy and healthy."

"Really?" she said. She hadn't spent much mirror time in rehab, though she did feel like none of her clothes fit.

"Don't listen to him, Chloe," Carrie said, defending her. "You're still practically see-through."

"I think he meant it as a compliment," Mikela said, smacking her own ample hips. "Not every chick in L.A. is fat free."

DJ Ray stepped up with more flowers for Chloe and hugged her in the way that boyfriends hug girlfriends. Chloe didn't want to drag him into her spotlight before she was sure they had something real, and definitely Chip's menacing presence didn't help make the timing feel right, so she whispered into his ear, "I can never thank you enough. I want to see you when I get back from my Magdalena tour. *Alone.*"

He smiled and stepped off, mouthing, "It's a date."

Chloe had to tear herself apart from us to do hand-in-hand interviews with Simone for all the assembled media. At this rate, did Magdalena even *need* to release the actual commercials?

PART Two

After

CHAPTER **15**

Malled

BUT MAGDALENA DID, in fact, air the actual commercials, the day after Chloe exited rehab, all over MTV. The ratings for *Laguna Beach* and *TRL* had never been so sky high, prompting speculation that kids were tuning in more for the ads than for the shows themselves. Would MTV have to pay to get the commercials instead of the other way around? Soon enough.

For Chloe's first big post-rehab personal appearance—at which *her* personal appearance became the topic du jour—Chloe and Simone met up at the Beverly Center to be driven in a lavender limo all the way from L.A. to the Mall of America. That's in Minnesota.

So soon after rehab, the idea of my girl riding off into the sunset side-by-side with Simone didn't go over well with me—Chloe wasn't supposed to do drugs, and Simone was a walking pharmacy. Sure, Chloe couldn't do anything alcohol- or drug-related on camera anyway, but there were a lot of gas stations between L.A. and Bloomington, and I was sure the cameras wouldn't be rolling *all* the time.

But Chloe had already reassured me that there was absolutely nothing to worry about.

"Nicole, I know you think Simone's the ultimate bad influence on me," she said, "and I know she's more of a bad thing than she is a good thing. Admitting that Simone is a problem is the first step, right?"

Chloe still didn't see Simone as being quite the manipulator that a few of us knew her to be, but at least she knew to keep her guard up.

The girls hopped into the limo with matching Chihuahuas (apparently, viewers were supposed to believe these were their cherished personal pets, but they were strictly accessories that might as well have had Burberry patterns on them) and huge grins. Then the limo took off.

By the time they would arrive in Bloomington several days later, several things had changed.

First, the commercials were airing pretty much nonstop. Viewership data showed that the ads piqued the interest not only of the hot-button eighteen to thirty-four age group, but of teens, tweens, children, and yes, even toddlers. Did you even know that they have ratings for what children starting as young as *two years old* watch and enjoy? How do you think the experts determine this? Toddlers can't work the TV on their own and at two, they'd probably enjoy *The Daily Show* as much as *Sesame Street* and *CSI*. But the data was conclusive—the Magdalena spots were quickly becoming a pop-culture phenomenon, and Chloe and Simone were a part of that ride.

MTV began airing the first half-dozen clips one after another, which added up to a short subject with a running time as long as the average music video. The ads showed them flanking Koi's sushi chef, laughing as Simone "accidentally" brought the seamless down behind them at their photo shoot, sharing a breezy lunch at Campanile that turned dramatic when Simone's ex-boyfriend was seated nearby (prompting her to shamelessly hit on the young Mexican waiter), and of course the infamous "very special ads" that took care to spotlight headlines of Chloe's mystery accident and eventual heartfelt turnaround in rehab. There's no question that both girls were becoming famous and that they had their fans among viewers and bloggers—if not necessarily among critics.

But fame is hungry. In the same way girls like to chase their sweet with a little salt, fame requires a misery chaser to every ounce of joy. For Chloe, the misery was about to meet her in front of Trinka's Trinkets at a mall large enough to house the entire population of a major metropolitan city.

On the road, Chloe sent me e-mails about rehab and about her reaction to seeing herself all over TV and in the tabloids. The e-mails often read like songs to me, so I would be sure to save them to send back to her later. One contained the line, "Now that I'm where I always wanted to be, I wonder where I'm going next." Top 40 would *kill* for that! I encouraged Clo to think of it as a song, and she was considering the idea as the limo pulled up to a throng of teenage girls outside the Mall of America.

"GTG!" she texted me. The next report would come hours later, after I'd already heard about some of the events from Carrie, an unlikely source.

Chloe and Simone had not spent the entire journey in the limo. As glam as a limo is, let's face it—after a few days in there, it would wind up kind of gross and littered with food and garbage. So after some good filming, the crew would stop at a suitably posh hotel for a little R&R, the girls would get their pick of clothing changes, and the limo would be swapped out with a fresh new one. Viewers almost had the impression that the trip had been nonstop, but that wasn't the only fake thing about that reality show.

Off-camera, Simone ignored Chloe. She spent all her time inventing ways to attract the crew's undivided attention, wisely deducing that anything outrageous would lead to air time. Looking stupid on TV meant being on TV, so who cared about the stupid part? Chloe, however, wasn't wild about looking like a dunce and spent all her time trying to lay off anything that made the crew laugh and point.

Pulling up to the mall, Simone flipped open her solid-gold cell phone. It was the same you-couldn't-buy-it-even-if-you-could-afford-it Karat One that she had made infamous.

"I thought you lost that thing," Chloe said.

"I did," Simone replied, spilling out packets of eye-shadow as she worked the Karat. "I had to call the company and beg them for another one. This one can hold, like, twice as many pictures of naked people. Look—see?"

She showed Chloe a doozy. It was a picture of Simone and a girl that Chloe didn't know, neither of them wearing shirts, standing beside a guy Chloe instantly recognized as Bond Grossman, an actor who played a doctor on some TV show that everybody loved but struck Chloe as amazingly boring most of the time and kind of stomach-turning when it wasn't. He wasn't wearing a shirt either and had war paint or something all over his face and shaggy chest.

"This is part of, like, a series that's supposed to be . . . artistic," explained Simone as she thumbed through the pictures, which increasingly had less paint and more flesh. "I'm thinking of selling them to a British newspaper because they can show tits in the paper over there."

"Isn't Bond Grossman pretty much married?" Chloe asked.

"Yeah, but she's a total bitch and always away, so it's cool."

They air-kissed before remembering they were really starting not to like each other that much and stepped out into an event they would not soon forget. Simone exited the limo first, sans panties—oops!—and pulled Chloe out behind her before hugging her close when the cameras began to roll.

"Look at all these people," Simone said, counting

beats as the cameras rolled. "It's like . . . we *are* the American dream."

". . . or its worst nightmare," Chloe said, scene-stealing.

The girls were whisked to a table that had been set up in front of Trinka's Trinkets, a decidedly younger-skewing brand that had nonetheless caught Magdalena fever and promoted their appearance throughout the week. Chloe was astonished at the turn-out. Over 10,000 girls, their vicariously jazzed mothers, and a few Web-savvy adult-male loners shifted their weight from foot to foot in a line six-deep that wound from a few feet in front of the little table all the way through the mile-long mall and right out the door.

Sipping the cosponsor juice (Poland Springs or Diet Pepsi, take your pick) that they'd been provided and feeding their dogs Nilla Wafers, the universe's newest stars sat facing the throng, anxiously awaiting the moment when the burly security guys would open the ropes and begin escorting the crowd, fan by fan, past Chloe and Simone for them to autograph a Magdalena press shot and hand each a little gift baggie with Magdalena samples and a pamphlet about the horrors of drug abuse.

Simone looked busty in a skimpy Dress top, probably because she was employing a trick she'd taught Chloe when they were minors—"If stuffing won't work because your top is too little, wear two bras—strapless under and strappy right on top of it. Everything will be held in place and will look three times the real size." Chloe hadn't needed that advice once she filled out to a natural C. Now, carrying extra poundage, she actually had a sports bra on to keep from feeling like a pornstar in front of a crowd she knew would be made up of all ages. She wore a cute Marni top and vintage suede skirt Carrie had loaned her under duress, fearing it would be stretched if a person with actual hips wore it.

While the cameras filmed the fandemonium, including thunderous chants of "Chloe!!" and "Simone!", Chloe took a private moment to confer with her other, if not necessarily better, half.

"Simone," Chloe said, a bit overwhelmed, "what are we going to do about this?"

"I know," Simone said impishly. "We have hardly any black fans. I'll have to phone in to BET or date Chingy or something."

"No, I mean—how can we sit here and sign for every single girl?"

Astrid came up to the table with two giant boxes full of black Sharpies.

"Girls, you're obligated to sit here and sign for exactly 120 minutes. In that time, you will use up six markers apiece, and we will make a dent this big" (she allowed a space of about a half inch between her thumb and forefinger) "in this sea of people. After the 120th minute, the big boys will step in front of the table, and I will escort you back through Trinka's and into the guts of this mall from whence you came. There will be pizza for you on the bus."

"Pizza?" Simone sniffed. "I haven't eaten pizza since I was, like, nine. I don't think I could even digest it."

"Sounds good to me," Chloe said. After throwing up all the toxins her body had absorbed since puberty, she'd spent the last half of rehab gorging on Thai food, pasta, chocolate cake, and that yummy real-fruit yogurt. Oh, and don't forget s'mores night. Food was her anti-drug.

Chloe was enjoying her curves and going off-diet for the first time since childhood, so she planned to continue down this path until she couldn't fit down it— or until the show stopped taping, when it was her goal to take time off to consider the varied and often hastily assembled offers that were pouring in for her. At that time, she could think about doing something that her former cocaine diet had always supplanted—eating right and working out.

The Magdalena cameras swung around to zoom in on Astrid. As if on cue, Astrid clicked on the mic that was affixed to the lapel of her indigo suit jacket and turned to confront the living, breathing embodiment of the always dreamed about and rarely obtained perfect demographic. Astrid was getting used to this.

"Girls! Girls! Attention, please! You will now get your chance to come face to face with the *faces* of Magdalena: Chloe and Simone!"

The noise that followed was one Chloe would have to get used to. As menacing as the dull roar from a stadium

full of male football fans can be, there is nothing as unnerving as hearing a mallful of young girls shrieking in
unison. It's like, when men cheer or boo, they almost un-
consciously harmonize into one homogenous bass sound.
But girls shriek at totally random levels, decibels . . . *fre-
quencies.* Even though you know it's a positive feeling
they're expressing, their inability to control the sounds
they make gives you this sick feeling in the pit of your
stomach.

If they decided to channel their happiness into rage,
teenyboppers could decimate anything in their path.

"Jesus, do they think Usher is under the table or something?" Chloe wanted to know.

"Girls! Girls! Chloe and Simone have just been invited
to present at *The MTV Video Music Awards* next week!
How do you like those apples? Pretty cool, right?"

More otherworldly shrieking, and this time, Chloe's
was mixed in.

"Seriously? I didn't know that!"

Simone said, "Yeah. It's cool. It's no biggie."

The rope dropped, and the security guys (who were
being cloned minute by minute as they called for back-
ups) escorted the first few girls up to the Magdalena
icons.

The very first fan set the tone. Morbidly obese in non-
descript jeans and an I ♥ MINNEAPOLIS T-shirt with a
pink breast cancer ribbon pinned to it, her name was Elizabeth, and she was thirteen and a half years old. Her hair

was long and blonde and had split ends, but she had really cute makeup and an infectious smile, and her eyes were bugged half out of her head at the privilege of being the first fan in line.

"Oh, my God, you guys, I seriously love you both so much," she said in a voice hoarse from screaming. She talked like a waitress at a truck stop who was about to launch into a long believe-it-or-not story about why she was so late for work.

"That's cool," Simone said, cranking up the sunshine.

"Especially *you*, Chloe. I support you *so much* for what you went through." This was an unexpected development.

Chloe felt an unexpected surge of emotion. She also felt like she couldn't possibly deserve so much empathy from the world.

"Thank you, Elizabeth. I'm nothing without you."

That was the first time Chloe realized that her rehab stint, despite being something almost too frighteningly real for Magdalena, had endeared her to viewers of the commercials.

Hugs were not allowed, even if supposedly initiated by the stars, and pictures were forbidden, but Chloe broke both edicts, causing the line to move as slowly as FEMA. She just couldn't say no to any request. The autographing time *was* cut in half, though, considering no one really needed "Parker" or "Westlake" on their photos—it had been streamlined into a simple "Chloe &" signed by Chloe and a "Simone" signed by her sidekick.

As the 120 minutes dissolved, part of the line was roped off and told they would not make it up to get autographs before the event ended, leading to chaos as some of the dejected fans mobilized on the upper level to take pictures from the Food Court, and others crowded around the edges of the table to watch the lucky ones in front of them get their time with Chloe and Simone, the very coolest stars ever.

Toward the end of the signing, a familiar face approached Chloe. It belonged to an Asian woman in pigtails and an oversized Simple Plan T-shirt who was holding the hand of an older white woman as if she were her mother. It took Chloe a second, but then she knew this was definitely the same Asian girl who'd peppered her with questions at Mode the night of her blow-out with Chip and Ana. That seemed like a million years ago.

"Hey, am I on drugs or do I know you?" Chloe joked, brightening reflexively. Then she realized there was no positive reason for this reporter to have come all the way from L.A. and hidden out in a line of teenage girls. It could only spell trouble. And this time, she probably wasn't there to ask Chloe about her famous friend Nicole Richie's TV plans.

The reporter stuck her hand out for a businesslike shake, but her nerves betrayed her—she was a bit dazzled to be in Chloe's presence, just as she had been back at Mode.

"Good eye, Chloe. Liz Chan here with *Bitz*." She spoke like she might be arrested for solicitation, looking around to make sure Astrid was distracted before going on. "I'm sorry to do this to you, but you and Simone—Simone, love your top!—are the biggest thing since BrAngelina."

"Do what to me?" Chloe was thoroughly confused. Then she followed Liz's eyes down to the hand she was holding, up a track-marked arm and to a face, the face of the woman Liz was passing off as her adopted Anglo mother.

She wasn't Liz's father; he was Chloe's—Freddy James had reared his ugly head.

"Hi, baby," Freddy rasped.

Chloe was stupefied. She had not seen or had contact with her biological father in fifteen years. Her memories were of a struggling musician and a handsome face, handsome enough to make him a B+ roadie, anyway.

The man in front of her was nothing like even her sketchiest memories. The Freddy of today had aged rapidly, well beyond his fortysomething years. Tall, painfully thin, with unkempt hair that hadn't seen many combs or styling aids, Freddy had a face that was lined, pinched, and veiny. His blue eyes that had once danced with excitement while sizing up groupies were now pale and drooped with sadness. He wore a crusty, plaid, short-sleeved shirt and gray sweatpants (so not Juicy) and struggled to tug his sleeves over the battered skin on his arms.

"Dad . . . ?" Even as Chloe said it, it sounded alien. She knew this wasn't her father—Julius was her real father. But "Freddy" would not have been right either. Conflicted feelings played across Chloe's face, and the camera caught all of them in supercloseup. "What—what are you doing here?"

"Hi, Chloe's dad," Simone butted in. "I'm Simone. Nice to meet you. Your daughter's my best friend. Thanks for, like, making her."

Freddy kept his eye on the prize. "Chloe, it's Dad. I just wanted to come see you. See how good you turned out. You look . . . so pretty. You have my eyes!" He wagged an accusing finger at Chloe, as if she'd stolen them. "You're doing great. I watch you on MTV all the time."

"What are you doing here, though?"

"I live here, Chloe. I moved here a while back. I'm married." Scrawny fingers were produced from Liz's grip, undulating in front of Chloe to show off the world's cheapest wedding band. Was that *even* made from metal? Or was it plastic? It looked like it might be out of one of the machines at the arcade across from the signing.

Belatedly, Chloe stood and hugged Freddy in a perfunctory way, then examined his face closely.

"I'm just shocked. I haven't heard from you in so long." *Why did you never contact me? Do you know how long I desperately waited to hear from you before I made up my mind that I hoped I'd never hear from you again?*

"Well, Chloe . . ." Freddy said wistfully. "You can't choose your fathers . . . well, *you* did—with Julius. But I mean, you can't pick your *real* fathers."

"Julius *is* my real father," Chloe said. She hadn't meant it in a cruel way; it was just a fact. "Look, it's not that I don't want to see you or talk to you, but this is, to put it mildly, just a really, really weird time for me. You don't want all of this on TV."

Then it dawned on Chloe. Of *course* he wanted it all on TV. Why else would he have come? With a reporter, no less?

Chloe turned to seek Astrid's help and found the PR enforcer standing with Freddy's signed release form. Astrid looked a bit smug, almost like she was enjoying Chloe's discomfort, before reverting to a tight-lipped air that suggested more appropriately that this was, after all, *just business* and that Chloe needed to accept it.

"Chloe, how are you *feeling* right now?" Liz finally squeaked, holding her recorder up for an exclusive comment before any members of the local media could potentially realize what was happening.

Chloe looked at the recorder, at Liz, at Freddy, at Astrid, at the security blockheads, and at the next tier of girls waiting to take their turn before their time ran out and possibly before Chloe and Simone's fifteen minutes ran out.

"I feel like I've never been more secure about who my true friends really are," Chloe said. It was a great, deliberately vague statement. People watching the commercial it would be featured in—and this moment was a lock to be a part of one of the commercials—could read absolutely anything they wanted into it. Liz was creaming at the thought of her first cover story.

Chloe finished with a confident, "I feel . . . secure."

"And I feel pregnant," Simone said.

The Ultimatum

A LOT OF THE AFTERMATH of the Mall of America episode—Chloe's birth father appearing out of thin air, Simone semi-announcing a pregnancy—was filtered through Carrie to me. Carrie had commented on the events for *Access Hollywood*, giving fairly intimate insights about Chloe's history with the Parkers and with Freddy, including an ill-advised and unauthorized airing of the tambourine story.

I like to think that Carrie did all of this commentary from a good place—her tone was definitely of defending Chloe and questioning Freddy's motives. But she also did it to get her face on TV, and without Chloe's knowledge, so I can see why Chloe declared her persona non grata for a little while. Carrie asked me if that was a band or something. When I explained the concept, she was pretty remorseful.

The very next issue of *Bitz* was a split cover with the headline REALITY BITES—Simone's picture was up top with the dramatic declaration, "Who's the father?" and Chloe's was right underneath with, "Who's the real father?" The article carried extensive commentary from Freddy, who'd undoubtedly been paid a tidy sum for dishing dirt on his suddenly famous daughter. It wasn't anything nasty; it was just personal information that gave fans something to jaw about. Plus an anonymous source had dished so much detail about the filming of the commercials and Chloe's reaction to Freddy that Chloe told me it was as if she'd been the source *herself.* Julius was apoplectic and wanted to sue, sue, sue, but Chloe later confessed to me in a midnight call that she had no intention of prolonging the incident by trying to go after Freddy.

"What am I gonna do? Sue Freddy for telling the truth?" Chloe reasoned. "Someone should sue Magdalena for doing the opposite."

But it's not as if the whole thing just rolled off her back.

"The thing is it was really . . . devastating to see this man," Chloe told me, "to actually *see* the man I sort of remember from when I was a little kid, but who I haven't seen or heard from ever since. Peggy and Julius adopted me, and I know it wasn't like there was an open invitation for Freddy to come hang out by the pool with us or anything, but it's not like there was a restraining order either. So he spent all this time not even trying to contact me or to see if I was okay. It took MTV to let him know I was alive, and his reaction was, 'I'll go see her and make some money off her.'"

Freddy took the somewhat ill-gotten money and went back to his own life. Only time would tell if he would reemerge at a later date, seeking more cash. If he did, maybe then Chloe would worry about holding a grudge. But Chloe can't stay mad at people for long, in the same way people can't seem to stay mad at *her* for any length of time.

Also, rehab makes a *huge deal* out of forgiving, and Chloe was like the star pupil of rehab. So it's not like she was going to obsess over Freddy's unfortunate and self-motivated appearance.

"I can't get all Jennifer Aniston about it," she told me. "He *is* my biological father. That's a fact. Now that he's done something kind of gross, I can't let it bother me because I'm not the one living in Minnesota with a drug problem and God only knows what else. I'm just . . . I'm just happy, really. I've got a lot going on with Magdalena. And Nicole . . . I'm writing songs."

"That's what I like to hear," I told her. "When are you coming back? I want to read some."

She wasn't back in L.A. until after she and Simone starred in a celebrity fashion show and then made an appearance as presenters at *The MTV Video Music Awards*, both slated to happen in Miami. Then she had a quickie slumber-party event in Vegas. She was focusing on how much fun it would be to hang out with all the cool people she knew and even cooler people she didn't know yet at the *VMAs*.

At this point, Magdalena—the woman, not the company—was showing symptoms of getting cold feet. If Magdalena had absorbed Chloe's surprise drug rehab, feeling it was at least an anti-drug statement, she wasn't sure what to make of an itinerant white-trash birth father (Astrid was bullish on this) and Simone's potential out-of-wedlock pregnancy (on this point, Astrid was a bit squeamish herself).

Legend has it that meetings between Magdalena and her staff would drag into the early hours of the morning as they contemplated all the angles, ran all the options. They could walk away from their most popular Magdalenas ever to avoid any possible negative association with aspects of the girls' lives that were a bit too real for their reality-TV concept, *or* they could stay the course, embrace the controversy and hope that their brand emerged as a newly energized, white-hot must-have for edgy kids with deep pockets and every member of their copycat cliques.

Privately, Magdalena—without a trace of the drag-queen persona she usually wore like base or her infamous accent—told Chloe and Simone: "I want you two *young ladies*—" she said it like she had other words in mind—"to know that I am personally responsible for your fame. Em-Tee-Vee is asking us about retooling you into a series; I am authorizing your fattened paychecks, and I'm signing off on all those little expenses you're fobbing off on Astrid." It sounded like Simone was up to her old accounting tricks, getting Magdalena to unwittingly finance her high living. "I will accept extra parents, and I will allow a baby on board if you are willing to comment on how the father is someone you plan to marry, Simone. But the one thing that is a deal breaker is drugs. We are exercising our right to ask that you submit to drug tests—Astrid will administer surprise tests, and if either of you tests positive, you're out. Is all of that understood?"

The girls were picking out their *MTV Awards* frocks at the Miami Versace boutique on the scorching hot day before the show, with Simone gravitating to Elton John Versace while Chloe was all Elizabeth Hurley Versace. Simone's Karat One was on speaker as nervous clerks draped gorgeously garish gowns over their shoulders, trying to pretend they weren't hearing every word of this juicy conversation. Chloe and Simone exchanged glances, neither of them all that surprised that the cameras were *not* filming *this* little business conference call.

"I'm not the addict," Simone said cattily. It was all the more bitchy because she said it, like always, as if she had absolutely *no idea* it was the most viciously mean thing she could have said at that moment. Chloe wondered how on earth Simone would pass even a single test. "So I'm not taking any pee tests. Talk to my lawyer. Oh, yeah—and I'm not pregnant after all, so don't worry about that, either."

"You're not?" Magdalena's accent and persona were

back. "Woooonderful! We'll issue a press release, and you can talk about it on the red carpet at the awards."

Chloe had never really believed that Simone might be pregnant. It wasn't like she didn't get around on the road despite their hectic schedule, but Simone's preferred activity with guys she considered one-offs was not likely to result in pregnancy—she was more in danger of getting a bad case of trench mouth than of finding herself in the family way.

"I'm clean, Magdalena," Chloe chimed in. "And I'm grateful for the opportunity Magdalena has given us. You'll never know how grateful. I've learned so much from this . . . experience. I'm happy to take the tests. I'm off drugs forever, so I'm not afraid to prove it."

At that moment, a salesgirl nonchalantly handed Chloe the dress that she just *knew* was *the* dress for her. It was a spectacular magenta halter-top gown with a gold buckle, plenty of space for her temporary hips and absolutely no back from shoulder to ass. It was so Versace, so Miami, so MTV, so Chloe.

"I'll take *that*," she said to the clerk, pointing at the dress.

"All right, girls—tomorrow, go show Miami and Em-Tee-Vee what being a Magdalena girl is *really* all about! And as for later today, make sure that little fashion show debut goes smoothly! I'm counting on you to do well for my good friend. He's the best designer in the world."

CHAPTER 17

Frockin' Out

A NOT-SO-FUNNY THING happened on the way to the *MTV Video Music Awards*—Simone Westlake got her ass fired by Magdalena.

After ordering up Versace gowns for their legit MTV debut, Chloe and Simone were whisked to a gaudy boutique that recently opened on Ocean Drive by down-but-returning fashion queenpin Guido Cavalieri. Guido had been a major influencer of style in the 1960s: the first to hire Twiggy, the first to introduce a bikini with fur on purpose, the first to issue a worst-dressed list, the first to popularize runway shows that made use of trendy music and a carnivale atmosphere, and the first to fire Twiggy.

Guido Cavalieri's signature look had a box-of-Crayolas feel, except less organized. You know, like the colors didn't gradually go from complementary to contrasting; opposite colors would throb and vibrate as next-door neighbors. There was no need to buy matching components of any Cavalieri outfits because none of them matched anyway.

Time had not been kind to Guido, who found his perhaps too-colorful offerings were providing inventory to most of the second-hand stores in existence for the next three decades. But over the past few years, the flamboyant Italian—known for always wearing impeccably tailored, if not foppish, clothes topped off by the worst rugs in history—had enjoyed a comeback, fueled not by critics or consumers, but by a deep-pocketed and clueless investor dead-set on returning Guido to fashion's fore with his seemingly random approach to fashion.

Guido and Magdalena practically went back to Biblical times together, so it was no surprise she'd promised him that her stars would be at his disposal for a major fashion show, set to occur right outside his storefront.

Maybe people know this by now after countless boring TV specials on the subject, so I guess it won't knock you over to read this, but the fact is, fashion shows are *not* very glamorous.

Clothes are wonderful, and magical, and transforming, but showing them off is a crazy freak show where puny tyrants scream at insanely tall, skinny women. Tell me what's so glamorous about being half-hidden, half-naked behind a half-curtain at a mall with people taping your breasts together?

Guido's storefront was attached to this mall, except it

didn't look like most malls. It was outdoors, had a koi pond, and a fountain and bougainvillea cascading from the railings surrounding the shops on the second level. All other details were temporarily obliterated by the mobs of shrieking young girls (there was that sound again) who had amassed on every square inch of space beyond the backstage area. A diaphanous half-curtain would flap freely each time someone walked in or out, affording the fans full-on views of Chloe, Simone, and a handful of unknown and yet seven-foot-tall Amazon models, as naked as the day they were born.

"Can they *see* us?" Chloe asked nervously as a pair of hands—two hands, not from the same person—hoisted a fluorescent green halter over her breasts.

Guido chuckled. "Silly young girl. Of *course* they can. A Guido show is very open, very free—we don't have limits. Fashion bows to no rules. You beautiful creatures *will* help make my name again."

Chloe felt like the most exotic animal at a small town zoo the way he was speaking to her. "We'll try," she said. She was being a trouper, but was no Mikela when it came to running around in the buff in front of elderly men.

Simone wouldn't shut up about the humidity. "This is why I stay away from Miami. Look at my hair. It's so flat." It looked pretty much the same to Chloe as it always did, but she didn't feel like taking the bait.

As showtime edged ever closer, the girls' Chihuahuas were making sweet love in the corner—whoever had thought it would be a great idea to get the girls one of each sex was probably a cat person—and over three dozen assistants were swarming Chloe and Simone, trying to help but just making matters worse and more uncomfortable.

Astrid entered the backstage area and immediately barked that the offending half-curtain needed to be nailed to the floor if it was going to flap in the breeze like that.

"These girls are not to be naked, nude, or unclothed!" she snapped at Guido as she approached. She had a slight runaway-train quality to her when she got going, Chloe noticed.

"It's only in fun," Guido begged. "The young girls enjoy a peek at the backstage life. . . ."

"So do the old perverts. No. N-O," Astrid said. Turning to the Magdalena cameras, she informed the lead cameraman that if any of the footage of Chloe and Simone in their "birthday suits" ever ended up *anywhere*, she would personally hunt him down and make him scream. He nodded and continued filming, trying to think of how to smuggle the footage out to interested buyers without getting caught.

"Guido, I've already done reconnaissance on this *mall* you're in. You'd think that here in the land of butt-floss bikinis, they wouldn't be as puritanical as a proud spinster like me, right? If so, then you'd be *wrong*. Dead *wrong*." Here, Astrid took a long drag from an already-lit cigarette handed to her by an executive assistant and then blew smoke out of her mouth and nose. "They keep reminding us that there can't be any nudity. On top of any local ordinances, I can tell you right now—and you're a dear friend of hers so I shouldn't have to—that Magdalena abhors nudity. Abhors it. The woman hasn't been nude herself since before these girls were born. Understand, Guido?"

Guido nodded. He'd been in the business long enough to expect to have the final word, but long enough to know when that was not going to happen.

"Why are you telling us this?" asked Simone, displaying a surprising attention to what was currently under discussion. "This is a *fashion* show. The *point* is the clothes. Why would we be naked?"

Chloe had to agree. The last thing she would do is allow herself to be seen naked for no good reason. Mikela would thrash her for not getting paid to do it. But she appreciated Astrid's concern for her privacy—and respected the thinly veiled warning. What she didn't respect quite so much was her embarrassing outfit. The show was filming this event as if Guido constituted what was hip in the world of fashion, as if these were clothes a Magdalena girl like Chloe would wear. He wasn't, and they weren't, and she wouldn't. The camera doesn't lie—but she was about to.

Astrid looked at Guido and then at both Chloe and Simone, studying their heads as if she were looking for words to be written there. Then she said solemnly, "I've just been asked to relay to you that there is to be no nudity. Can you all reassure me of that?"

It was time for a response à trois—they yessed her in

unison, and she seemed satisfied, leaving to take her place in the front row of a little fashion show Miami would not soon forget. Chloe immediately texted me the lowdown. If only she'd read my response—I predicted exactly what would happen next.

After all the prep, Chloe felt a little bit like a Miss Universe contestant in her home country's native outfit—you know, larger than life and about three inches tall at the same time, plus sweaty. She was the first person expected to go down the rickety runway, which was surrounded on all sides by teenagers whose idea of fashion was a sale at the Gap. As she stood awaiting her cue, all Chloe could think of was how drugged up she would normally have to be to walk on a stage and be inspected by a sea of eyes, especially in a tacky outfit like the one she was being paid to wear. Her nerves evaporated when she realized that this experience was not going to make or break her—she would just swallow any misgivings she had and soldier onward.

"And now, let the show begin!" shouted a triumphant Guido from the main stage. He raised his arm and waved a red cape, as if the crowd should expect an out-of-control bull to barrel down the runway from behind the curtains. Instead, Chloe snapped the curtain aside—she practically had to tear it down thanks to the nails decreed by Astrid—and strode out, waving to the wall of noise that greeted her. The fans were screaming so wildly and there was so much commotion, she almost forgot she was in what amounted to a green bra, purple bicycle pants, a white train, and six-inch spiked red heels. Her hair had never been so high on her head, and her face was so thick with Magdalena product, the pores would never unclog. But she knew that underneath it all, she was okay.

Chloe made it to the end of the runway, did an exaggerated catwalk turn, and returned, laughing and enjoying herself. She passed a high five to Simone as she made her way back to the curtain. Simone was no better off than Chloe, wearing an orange T-shirt paired with a blue floor-sweeper skirt and a green, sombrero-like hat.

Nobody ever said Guido was a *good* designer, just a famous one.

But Simone, see, was never really sold on being confident in who she was or on letting the clothes do the talking. She was not enjoying being someone's sidekick, and she could never leave well enough alone.

When Simone got to the end of the catwalk, and with all eyes on her, she very slowly and very deliberately flipped her T-shirt up and hooked it over her head, revealing her breasts for all the world to see. For a second, everyone made no noise at all. Then a chorus of cheers, boos, and laughter shook the entire mall.

Astrid Dillinger sat as stiff as a three-day-old corpse in her front row seat, studying the nipples so rudely paraded before her face and after her dire warning.

"I told them no nudity," she said to a flabbergasted Liz Chan, who sat next to her, feverishly taking notes for *Bitz*.

Astrid said it in the same tone a proud father might use to tell a fellow audience member, "That's my boy!" of his son during a school play. But Astrid was anything but proud. It's just that her emotions hadn't caught up with her vocal chords. When they did, there would be hell to pay.

CHAPTER  *18*

Reality Sinks In

IT HAD ALL HAPPENED so quickly that Chloe's head was spinning—and she was sober.

Chloe was seated in the cavernous back end of the lavender limo, an increasingly familiar spot for her. She was perfectly spray-tanned, tastefully Versaced, her hair loose and romantic with just a touch of Magdalena product between her face and the world this time—in all the confusion leading up to the *MTV Video Music Awards*, she had been able to do her own makeup for a change.

The glaring omission was the absence of Simone in the seat beside her. In place of Simone, seated across from Chloe and wearing DKNY and a frown was Astrid Dillinger, her new professional babysitter.

Simone's stunt had proved once and for all there really *was* such a thing as bad publicity.

Going topless may have delighted the photographers present and some of Simone's more nonconformist fans, but most of the Magdalena faithful—and the public at large, including the star-bashing media—had found it to be a disgusting act of shameless self-promotion. Well, okay, the *whole* Magdalena thing was shameless self-promotion. But engaging in shameless self-promotion *topless*—that was an areola too far. The headlines had not been teasing and tantalizing; they'd been brutal and rude, alluding to the empress having no clothes and a "flat" tax on Magdalena products.

Chloe hadn't seen Simone after the fashion show. Instead, she'd received a phone call from Astrid late that night to inform her that she was invited to continue on solo—no more Magdalena Girls, just one Magdalena Girl.

"Okay," Chloe had said numbly to Astrid. The business advisors hastily gathered by Peggy with a little help from Julius were in agreement that the development could only be positive for Chloe—and that she'd have to be "on drugs" not to take it. Of course, part of the arrangement was that she reaffirm her vow to willingly submit to spot-checks to prove she *wasn't* on drugs.

"Okay, Astrid. I understand."

"And are you prepared to do the commercials alone? And the awards show?" Astrid had asked. "With no relapses, right?"

Chloe agreed. "Yes, Astrid. You can count on me." *I can count on me.*

And so there she was, a former ballerina about to return to the stage, sitting across from Astrid, as tough a critic as any alive.

Chloe had been asked to present an award in the newly added category of Most Stylish Video, and the nominees were A-list names with serious music careers—all talented people Chloe would love to trade places with. It's not that she envied their talent; it's that she envied that they'd already done the hard part—*started*. The little songs Chloe had been writing as poems were piling up in her clutch, but she was more nervous than ever about what she would do with them next. She knew she could always ask her father for help—but he had sworn off helping her back when she was high 24/7. Maybe he had changed his mind?

The lavender limo pulled up outside the American Airline Arena—whatever happened to prestigious-sounding names like Madison Square Garden or Wembley?—and Chloe took a deep breath. She would probably be the only dateless person there. Even the closeted stars had beards. Chloe had Astrid, who in the right light could pass for at best a mustache.

The driver came around and opened her door, and Astrid awkwardly clambered over Chloe to get out first. Chloe could tell by the expression on Astrid's face that the red carpet (actually, it was white—welcome to Miami) must look like a jungle. She stepped out, mustering all the grace under pressure that she could.

If you've never been to an awards show, in some ways,

they're like going to the grocery store. You see all these famous stars like familiar brands, and they're arranged side by side so you don't know where to look first. You have unlimited choices—Do you want to watch Gwen and Gavin because they're Hollywood royalty? Try to meet Avril and Deryck since they're young and edgy? Watch to see what kind of diva stunt Mariah Carey has up her nonexistent sleeve? Or park near the entry and go gown surfing, ogling all the outfits as they file past regardless of whether they're being worn by the A, B, or C list or the A, B, or C cup? Decisions, decisions.

The *MTV Video Music Awards* were Chloe's first-ever carpet of any color as a star, so she was taking it all in with unbridled enthusiasm. Sure, she'd grown up around the rich and famous, so she knew some of these stars, but she'd always just been on the periphery; she'd been Julius and Peggy's little girl in the party dress, dancing behind her parents. Now, she was a grown woman with rehab under her Versace belted halter dress and a red-hot reality project that was making her a household name.

When this story first began, Chloe would have made a piss-poor role model, but she was now flush with the knowledge that thanks to turning her life around, she was becoming someone any young girl could look up to and was distancing herself—at least privately—from the human guilty pleasure that was Simone.

There was almost no white of the white carpet left in

sight. In its place were hundreds of celebrities of every stripe, their latest flings, their fake spouses, their publicists, security men, and probably a few skillful crashers. Both sides of the carpet were choked with event photographers, stacked practically on top of one another in sloppy rows, all craning over the barricades in an effort to get the best possible shots of each subject.

When Chloe made her way down the carpet, it was nothing like the times she'd accompanied her parents. She was no one's guest—she was a star.

"Astrid?" she whispered as she began the journey.

"Yes?" Astrid replied, absorbed and awed by the endless line of print and TV reporters standing between them and the front door.

"I've seen this a million times—just from a different angle. You're gonna take me from reporter to reporter, say my name, and if they ask a weird question, pull me away to the next one. Got it?"

For once, Astrid was taking orders from someone other than Magdalena.

"Check."

Chloe felt like a sponge tossed into an ocean. The water was a mixture of adulation from fans who'd gathered just out of reach and an animalistic need for interaction radiating from every member of the press she was paraded past. After posing for both banks of demanding and demeaning paparazzi (several made loud references to the fact that she was alone) and therefore allowing her Versace perfection to be captured forever, Chloe was escorted by an uncertain Astrid down the never-ending line.

"Hi, Chloe. Not going topless tonight?" from *Radar*.

"Chloe—why couldn't you get a date?" from *People*.

"Do you find being heavier a plus or minus in bed?" from *Cosmo*.

"What was your lowest moment . . . y'know . . . on drugs?" from *Time*.

"What's your, like, favey-fave color?" from *Tiger Beat*.

The questions started out like these and got worse. Chloe deflected them with every ounce of charm her father had instilled in her or cast them down with every ounce of sass from her mother. A few questions were legit, and she was able to answer them with poise, including one from *Rolling Stone* about whether it was true that she had musical aspirations—that one was a big yes!

When she got to that intrepid Liz Chan from *Bitz*, she couldn't even pretend. Astrid insisted she answer some questions from *Bitz* since they had provided so much coverage of the commercials already, but Chloe wondered if she was supposed to act grateful for the kinds of headlines that got cut-and-pasted into e-mails and traded among friends for a laugh.

"Chloe, you're the new 'It' girl," Liz said.

"That's not a question," Chloe said curtly.

Liz smiled nervously. She was sopping wet with perspiration in her off-the-rack prom gown and clearly seemed almost not to recognize what a bottom-feeder Chloe felt her to be. "Sorry, yes. First question: How does it feel to go from making commercials to being the star of your own reality TV series?"

Chloe was dumbstruck. "Come again?"

"Your own show. I know it's not officially announced yet, but we at *Bitz* are hearing rumors that the Magdalena reality commercials are set to become, you know, like a real *show*. On MTV2."

Chloe stared Liz down for a full ten seconds as she contemplated whether to deny it and challenge her or roll with it and say it's an honor. She darted her eyes to Astrid, who was of no help—she just looked back at Chloe expectantly.

"Well, Liz," Chloe said, recovering her footing, "I guess you'll just have to stay tuned for that. Have a great evening—I need to go do my Joan Rivers interview now." It was the first time a star had used Joan Rivers as a safe haven, but Chloe had met Joan many times and so could bask in the glow of compliments about growing up nicely.

Between *Bitz* and Joan, Chloe managed to ask Astrid, "What's she talking about?" Astrid whispered back, 'We'll talk." "Bitch!" Joan Rivers teased. "That's my line!"

Post-Joan and once Chloe was whisked to the decidedly less glam backstage—visions of the cinderblock halls of her youth, when Liv would drag her from dressing room to dressing room, danced in her head—Chloe was penned up in a makeshift green room, where she was supposed to wait for her cue to go onstage and present the first award of the evening, Most Stylish Video. She sat with Astrid on a kinda stinky, rust-colored couch, eating stale popcorn from a large bowl. Various production people whizzed about, in and out of the room, as did some actors and singers of varying degrees of fame.

"So Astrid," Chloe said, "let's chat. What's up with the rumor about the commercials becoming a show?"

"It's true," Astrid said flatly. "We just haven't gotten around to telling you yet."

"Haven't gotten—?" Chloe didn't know whether to pee in excitement ("My own show!") or smack Astrid's face in anger ("How could the press know before me?"). She chose the middle ground. "You need to communicate with me and stop treating me like I'm some new body mist you're developing. I need to know that stuff, so I don't look like an airhead on the red carpet. My own show? Really?"

"Really," Astrid said, ignoring the smack-down part. "The kids are eating you up, your ups and downs. Older girls aren't wild about you since you're—you know—kind of silly to them. But their little sisters are loving you. And they're at that age when consumer loyalty is built."

Silly? Chloe didn't like the sound of that. But she liked the sound of her own show. Maybe Magdalena would lay off a bit and film more genuine things. Maybe she could have Joey play on the show, and she would showcase her new poems as songs.

The only down side would be she'd really have to watch herself and not pull a Simone—being a corporate shill usually comes with some kind of morals clause, but being the star of an MTV2 show practically comes with an immorals clause. What was good for your brand may not be so good for a young, hip, discriminating TV audience. From then on, Chloe would have to straddle that line or risk losing it all.

"Have your people talk to my people," Chloe said, wondering if she could truly handle being the focus of a reality show.

"I *am* my people," Astrid replied dryly. Just then, David Spade stuck his head in and said, "You're next."

Astrid handed Chloe over to some pretty young coke-whores in strapless, sequined numbers, who in turn escorted her to the stage entrance, where booming laughter and miked up monologues were reverberating. She couldn't hear anything clearly, but Chloe could see on the screen some choice Magdalena moments being replayed, all of her least faves, the ones that really brought out her stupid side. Except most of them were engineered moments, so the stupidity was far removed from her behavior on even her blondest days. They culminated with a blurry screen grab of Simone lifting her Guido Cavalieri top, with her own top obscured by black boxes.

So much for a tasteful introduction.

When Chloe's name was called, she walked out onto the stage and into a trap she never saw coming. Her only rehearsal for the show had been done using stage notes in her hotel room—her Magdalena handlers including Astrid had mandated that she not be seen in public after yesterday's incident and Simone's firing, not until her Manolos touched white carpet. So Chloe had lived in a bit of a bubble the past twenty-four hours. No more—the bubble burst with a loud, sickening BANG.

As she waltzed over to the podium, all ready to read some names and present a winner with a moonman, a trickle of boos greeted her from the audience. As unnerving as adolescent shrieks of delight can be, guttural adult boos suck pretty hard, too. Chloe had always been rock royalty, right? How could her peers—or at least her father's peers—give her such an *un*welcome?

Chloe kept trying to tell herself the boos could be downplayed when the show was aired, and it's not like *everyone* was booing. But she learned in that ten-second walk from backstage to onstage, there is a big difference between real rock royalty and Middle America—stars are *not* your fans, and these particular stars were not impressed with the overnight sensation who'd ridden a lavender limo to fame, accompanied by a recently shirtless she-devil.

Chloe was beginning to cry before she realized it and was mad as hell that her body, her tear ducts, had betrayed her. She was misting up big-time and couldn't help it—the boos killed her buzz, made her doubt what right she had to be there, and made her wonder if she deserved them. You can't deny boos from an arena—they are a consensus. She wished she was leaving on an American Airlines jet plane.

At the mic, Chloe cleared her throat and wondered

how she could speak without sobbing. Instead, she surprised herself by laughing. The sound of her own laugh killed the waterworks and helped to quell some of the groans from the audience.

"You know," she said, her voice shaky at first, but firmer as she went along. "Magdalena's eyeliner is waterproof, but if y'all don't lay off, we'll really put it to the test." The boos died down, and a few people cheered. One person screamed, "I love you, Chloe! You rock!"

Chloe smiled, defusing the moment. "Thank you, but even *I* know I don't rock, not really, not like the great bands here tonight. Not *yet*. Right now, I'm just rolling along. I'm having fun—on TV anyway." Some laughter. Going off-script can pay huge dividends as long as you're not taunting the FCC. "I'm not here to fake cred as a rock star, and I'm not here to take off my clothes. I'm not even here to sell you some makeup. I'm here to tell you that the nominees for Most Stylish Video—a subject I actually *do* know something about—are . . ." From then on, she dutifully read the TelePrompter.

By the time she was all finished, Chloe had won over all but the most diehards in the audience. She received hearty hugs from the metal band that claimed the award (metal bands would hug anyone with cleavage) and was able to hold her head high as she left the stage.

Chloe had gone it alone, despite her doubts. Maybe she *could* handle her own reality show. As long as it balanced the right amounts of "reality" and "show." Right?

As she made her way offstage, a familiar face entered her field of vision. It was DJ Ray. Ray was in Armani (keep in mind Chloe had never seen him in anything but old T-shirts and ratty jeans, the official uniform of DJs) and looked like a movie star. I'm not saying DJ Ray is perfect because nobody is, but I'll say this: The boy has good timing.

"Ray!" Chloe shouted. It was loud enough that her voice would have to be edited out when MTV aired the ceremony. Which was okay because Astrid was already making sure MTV promised to soften the boos and edit Chloe's brave appearance to tease it for maximum positive impact.

"Hey," Ray said, smiling with this suave look that said, "What, you weren't expecting me?"

"I can't believe you're here!" Chloe couldn't stop herself from hugging him even though they'd never shared anything like that before. It's like their romance started during the time they were apart and had been amping up in their minds. Now, face to face, they were picking up where their relationship had already progressed to mentally.

Chloe hugged Ray again, pressing her face into his neck to inhale his scent—she wanted to drink in this entire moment—as Astrid and two security guys approached, impatiently waiting to drag her from Point A (the stage) to Point B (the after party, where she was expected to make an appearance).

"I can't believe you didn't call me to tell me you'd be

here," Chloe said. "Are you working the after party or something?"

Ray shrugged. "No, I'm actually not here on business at all. And if I called you to tell you I was coming, then . . . it would have ruined what I was doing. I came here to surprise you."

Chaos reigned around them as presenters, winners, security, and P.A.s hustled back and forth. "Chloe, we need to *go*," Astrid hissed.

But there was a calmness in the bubble created by Ray and Chloe's embrace. She stared into Ray's dark brown eyes. They were gleaming, darting back and forth as they stared back at Chloe. This was what people meant when they said that a person's eyes could sometimes communicate much more than simple words. In Ray's eyes, Chloe saw something she'd never seen before—genuine and unselfish love for her.

"Ray . . . I don't know what to say."

"Sure you do," Ray encouraged. "Just say the first thing that comes into your mind. That's usually the most honest."

Chloe didn't think about it; she just said it. "I love you for coming tonight. I'll never forget it."

"You can see her at the *after* party," Astrid said, taking Chloe by the wrist and leading her away. "Come on, Chloe—we have a contract. . . ."

As Chloe left, she suddenly realized that she had *kind of* just told Ray, who she'd never even been out on a date with, that she loved him. Was that . . . too fast? She looked back over her shoulder to make sure he got the message to find her at the after party, and as she did, she saw Ray still hadn't broken their eye contact. "Me, too," he mouthed.

Official after parties are no party.

You're expected to be there *and* be square—it's all about showing up, being photographed ad nauseum, talking with whatever media outlet has the exclusive, and then leaving in time to go to the really juicy parties. But Chloe would always remember the *MTV Video Music Awards* after party because she danced the entire night with DJ Ray, and they shared their first kiss in a shadowy corner before she had to leave for the airport. She was heading to Las Vegas, but Chloe felt she'd already gambled on a romance with Ray and won.

Maybe she should have quit while she was ahead.

CHAPTER 19

What Happened in Vegas

MY REUNION WITH CHLOE was bittersweet—
chocolate, that is. We were scarfing down cookies from a
tarnished silver tray left behind after some gross conven-
tion in a room just off the lobby of the Sinbad Resort &
Casino in Las Vegas. Chloe hadn't been back to Vegas
since her days as a child prostitute, and here we were, already up to no good again—looting. If we got caught by
the hotel staff, our defense was going to be that we were
just looking for food. We were, actually, and we'd found it.
What girl can resist a chocolate-chip cookie or three to
munch while your absolute best friend is filling your brain
with gossip galore?

Chloe looked good. She'd lost a few of her Promises
fifteen pounds, but not so many that her face was in danger of heading back to the sallow addict look. She was still

in her Versace, which she'd slept in on a private jet chartered to get her from Miami to Vegas so that she'd be able to host a hastily thrown together celebrity slumber party—all for the Magdalena cameras to film, of course. They were running out of footage to use after blowing their wad on the controversial, "Sometimes friends go too far . . . and then it's time to get new friends" spot, which showed Simone going too far and getting booted. Now that the commercials were morphing into an actual series, they needed more, more, more.

"Do you think Simone will ever forgive me?" Chloe asked, but she didn't seem too concerned about the answer.

"Let's hope not," I said. "Now tell *all* about Ray."

This was a rare moment for Chloe—being alone with a friend and with Astrid nowhere in sight. Astrid had checked them both in (Chloe's new fake name was Donna Martin—we approved) and looked the other way for ten seconds, long enough for Chloe to escape. She needed some alone time to digest everything that was happening to her at the speed of light. She filled me in on all the details of the Cavalieri fashion fracas, on her almost-disastrous awards appearance (I was so glad I wasn't there because I would have made such a scene from the audience once those posers started to boo her), and on Ray's amazing surprise. She wouldn't talk much about what it was like kissing Ray, saying it was such a new feeling for her that she wanted to savor it as long as possible. And then she told me how her series of little commercials were about to become an actual *series*.

In the jet on the way over, Astrid had informed Chloe that Magdalena was keen to accept the generous MTV2 offer to retool the commercials into a full-fledged reality show: *Magdalena Girl*. The theme song would be set to the tune of *Macarena*, something Chloe hoped DJ Ray would not hold against her, and the first episodes would consolidate all of the already-aired ads. Those wouldn't last long, and new episodes would be built around increasingly over-the-top events, the first of which would be the celebrity slumber party in Vegas. The slumber party had always been on the agenda, but it was supposed to be for fans with Chloe making a brief appearance to introduce a new night mask for teens. Now, all of Chloe's friends and just about any available female talent had been invited to show up in PJs to work a red carpet and party in the Sinbad ballroom at a slumber party that seemed to be about anything but actual sleeping—it would kick off at midnight, end at 6:00 A.M., and be filmed from every conceivable angle.

Chloe told me how she'd originally heard about the series idea from a reporter, which turned her off. But she had accepted the series and signed on the dotted line while on a conference call on the jet with her mom (who was coming to the slumber party, too), her business managers, and Magdalena herself. Astrid would probably be getting a nice, fat bonus for securing this deal—and don't forget that signing Chloe (and oh, yeah, Simone) had been Astrid's idea in the first place. If you did forget it, Astrid would remind you anyway.

Once she finished with the contracts, Chloe had to provide one more thing—some pee. Astrid sprang the first surprise urinalysis on Chloe. It made her uncomfortable and made her feel untrusted, but one thing it did not make Chloe feel was nervous—she hadn't done drugs in well over a month, and since they weren't testing for marijuana (which can stay in your body up to three months—or so I've heard), she knew she was peeing Evian as far as drugs were concerned.

After the signing, the jet had landed, and Chloe had sleepwalked through a deserted airport and into another lavender limo and finally trudged into the Sinbad, only to find me in the lobby.

"Clo," I said, "you know that doing this series means you'll have tons of opportunities put in front of you— movies, TV, music, fashion, ads involving the near-naked washing of cars . . ."

Chloe laughed. "I know. But I'm not in this for the quantity—I'm in it for the quality. That's my take on everything now. I'd be happy if I could get a recording deal out of this. Quality is the new black—that's why I finally called Chip and . . . you know . . . dumped him." We laughed at his expense. So long, Stinky.

"My only concern is that we stop doing so many phony things, you know? I told Astrid that, and I trust her to keep things as real as possible. That fashion show was the worst."

I wasn't so sure that banking on a reality show to end up real was a wise gamble, but I had learned my lesson about killing Chloe's buzz. I just told her I was proud—and I was.

"God, this hotel is so weird," Chloe said, looking around in disbelief. "I can't believe people pay to come stay here. It's so too-much. But it's so familiar to me—like, I can almost picture being here before . . ."

"Hey, girl!" Carrie and Mikela had found us. I'm not sure, but I think it's because Carrie can pretty much smell gossip from a mile away.

Chloe was ecstatic to see two more familiar faces. There's this big thing in rehab about how you're not supposed to reconnect with your old druggy friends, how the only way to stay out of the downward spiral is to completely disconnect with your old life. Chloe never quite bought it. It didn't make sense to her that one thing—not doing drugs—should keep her from a lifetime of stories, connections, and fun. Anyway, so many of our friends, both using and not, had been through rehab that all of them respected what it's all about.

Chloe had pretty much done drugs with everyone we knew at some point or another, so cutting all of them off would mean retiring from her life altogether, and she just wasn't willing to do it. And with the whole Magdalena thing, she was actually getting paid a lot of cash in part because of the glamorous friends she had in her life, so following the rehab's little edict would have meant quitting the only job she ever had—and that just wasn't going to happen.

Still, she wondered if she was putting herself at risk because seeing Mikela made her wonder how many Xanax were in her purse—even if she had no intention of bumming any.

"I'm so glad you guys came," Chloe said, hugging both of the newcomers.

"Even me?" Carrie asked. "I'm not still au gratin, am I?"

"It's persona non grata," I reminded her.

"No, you're not," Chloe said, laughing. "I'll forgive you. Just don't talk to the press again without asking me first. Things can get twisted around so easily. But I'm so grateful you both came here!"

"They *flew* us," Mikela said. "Not that we wouldn't have come anyway! But that purple Magdalena limo they brought us here in was a mistake. Some girls got out of their car at a stop light and screamed your name."

"Yeah!" Carrie added excitedly. Clearly, this had not been an inconvenience from her perspective. "They *rocked* the car! We didn't know what to do, so we rolled down the window and gave them a bag of makeup samples we found in the back."

"So what are you wearing tonight?" Mikela wanted to know. "I have this amazing yellow vintage Azzaro my mom's had since the 1960s. It's unreal."

Chloe laughed. "Sounds very shy. I'm not sure what I'm wearing, but Astrid is on it. I'm sure she'll get me some amazing designer negligee."

About twelve hours later, I was standing next to Chloe wearing the kind of amazing designer negligee she'd been dreaming of while she was wearing an eyesore—it was a hideous patchwork of colors that worked hard *against* each other. Since it was designed for sleep, it was kinda funny that it was such a nightmare. But then, it was also a signature piece by Guido Cavalieri.

"Astrid!" Chloe shouted. "I don't want to wear this! It looks terrible on me. People will think I really dress like this."

Astrid was in white silk men's pajamas with black piping. The bunny slippers were definitely from her personal collection. "Chloe, you signed a contract and part of that contract is to honor the contracts that Magdalena has in place—and our agreement with Guido Cavalieri is an important one. There is no discussion, Miss. You're wearing it. Now get out there and have fun. Just be yourself."

I took Chloe's hand and squeezed it. "You look good," I said. "It's the nightie that's ugly." We laughed, and I took her down a short hallway from the backroom we'd gathered in and out into the VIP area of the world's biggest slumber party.

The main ballroom of the Sinbad had seen serious action in its day. In the 1960s, it was rumored that Marilyn Monroe tried to throw herself over the ornate gold-gilt balustrade on the spiral staircase after being spurned by President Kennedy. In the 1970s, it was used for galas thrown by Hollywood's old guard, mob princes and princesses, and casino royalty. In the 1980s and 1990s, a televised dance competition was filmed there weekly.

And now, it was going to be the setting for a notorious meltdown, also captured by the cameras.

The ballroom, like the rest of the Sinbad, was decked out in a quasi-Middle Eastern theme, with huge urns in the corners and squat gold tables with genie lamps on them sitting over Persian rugs. Probably any person of actual Arabic descent would have barely recognized the influence, but then it wasn't authentic—that wouldn't be very Vegas.

That night, there wasn't a lot of room to inspect the decor since the place was hopping with half-naked girls in every imaginable type of sleepwear. You had your undiscovered starlets in Victoria's Secret (I don't know why they called it a secret because the cat was pretty much out of the bag), A-list stars in two-piece Arianne sets, and older connected ladies in more flattering formal nightgowns. Most sleepwear isn't designed to be seen by more than the person you're going to bed with, so there weren't as many markers to flaunt how pricy yours was, leading women to gild the lily with expensive accessories—borrowed jewelry, Prada slippers, and even a few tiaras.

Chloe was the only woman in Guido Cavalieri. The bright side? She definitely stuck out at her own slumber party.

The ballroom had been covered in enormous feathers, as if the world's biggest pillow fight had recently occurred, and pillows were strewn about or stacked on chairs. Sleeping bags suited for toddlers with Hello Kitty and Barbie motifs were draped over gaudy chairs. Punch bowls served actual punch, and a wealth of nutritionally unsound snacks were available, just like at a real slumber party— caramel corn, cookies, cake. It was going to waste with this crowd, most of whom hadn't eaten in forty-eight hours in preparation for being filmed in their PJs.

Chloe had no frame of reference for a classic slumber party. As a kid, the closest she came to this phenomenon was getting lost inside a friend's Beverly Hills mansion and not being discovered until it was too late to go home. She also should have had no frame of reference for the grand ballroom, and yet she felt she'd been in it before— she told me it must have reminded her of something from a bad acid trip she'd once been on.

The most obnoxious part of the celebrity slumber party would be the Jumbotron screens set up on each wall, which were showing footage of the event as it happened. The effect it had was to encourage partygoers to *not* act naturally and instead to spend lots of time waving at the screen and goofing off in hopes that the Magdalena crew would focus on them for a few seconds.

In our VIP area, there were already a lot of people we didn't recognize standing between us and the few people we did recognize. But no one would keep Chloe apart from her mom—Peggy had arrived and looked ravishing in an emerald silk number that covered everything up except for her natural grace.

"Mom!" Chloe shouted and darted over to her. They hugged and sat down to catch up.

"I'm so proud of you," Peggy said after a while. It's not that Chloe didn't know her mother's sometimes volatile behavior obscured a deep and lasting maternal love, but hearing Peggy say she was *proud* gave Chloe her highest post-rehab high yet.

"Thanks, Mom."

Don't worry—the cameras caught that. Just as the *Magdalena Girl* cameras caught all the bad stuff, like Chloe hyperventilating over her Cavalieri wardrobe, Chloe snoring in Versace on a chartered jet, Chloe snippily assessing all the PR-seeking no-names who'd accepted invites to her bra-and-panties party, the cameras also ate up all the magical moments. Chloe was so used to the crew, they didn't take anything away from intimate moments. But she had to realize that for every touching moment, the cameras—like fame itself—were hungry for an equal and opposite crazy moment.

"Where's Clayton? We almost missed this!"

The producer girl speaks! The girl who consistently directed all the camera's movements from Day One rarely made a peep, but she was apparently missing one of her cameramen. Not surprising since we were in a room full of women in their underpants.

"That's sooo sweet. The sweetest!" It was Liz Chan from *Bitz*—again. She's spied Chloe and Peggy holding hands and talking and decided it was as good a time as any to announce her presence. Thanks to Chloe's schedule, the reporter was racking up frequent-flyer miles and becoming harder to get rid of than body lice. Liz was wearing a pair of white pajamas with pink and blue flowers on them, straight out of the Sears catalog. That at least made Chloe feel a bit better about her own undesirable—but designer! designer!—duds.

"How did you get up here?" Chloe demanded. "Astrid, I want no press up here." Astrid came over, but didn't seem too keen on kicking out the press outlet that had given Magdalena the most coverage, even if some of it had been at Chloe's expense.

"I'm sorry; I don't mean to bother you," Liz said, snapping a pic of Chloe and Peggy with her trusty digital camera. "No Photographers" didn't necessarily mean no photography, not when a tabloid journo was involved.

"Then don't," Peggy snapped. "I don't know who you are, but if my daughter doesn't want you around, and *I'm* around, you better leave, or you'll regret it."

When Peggy was on Chloe's case, it was a drag. But when she turned her ferocity on someone threatening Chloe's peace of mind, it was like harnessing the power of a hurricane. It made Chloe feel so protected and loved. It made Liz Chan feel like wetting herself.

"Yes, ma'am," Liz said, shuffling off as quickly as her

slippers would let her. No sooner had one foe been taken care of than another appeared—Ana Cannon. Ana was wearing a pretty white lace nightgown but had tackily adorned it with safety pins to maintain her punk attitude. But even so, her outfit looked better than Chloe's.

Mikela and Carrie slipped behind Chloe protectively, forgetting for a moment to mug for the Magdalena cameras and instead wanting to make sure Chloe wouldn't snap and pick up where she'd left off with Ana back at Mode.

"Chloe!" Ana said with the excitement of a three-year-old being handed a lollipop. She rushed up to where Chloe sat and stooped to give her a great, big air kiss, affording Chloe and Peggy a bird's eye view of her powdered cleavage with its little bleeding-heart tattoo that peeked over her neckline. "Chloe! I'm so happy you invited me, and I'm so happy for you and your commercials—they're everywhere! I heard a rumor you might turn them into a show?"

"I *didn't* invite you, Ana," Chloe said, "but thanks for not letting that stop you. Mom, this is Ana Cannon. Ana, meet Peggy Parker."

Ana ignored the introduction and instead tried to get Chloe to come with her over to the cameras. "The guys wanted a picture of us together for *Us*," she said, as if she were just trying to satisfy their request.

"No, not now," Chloe snapped, annoyed that a photographer was let in. Oh, great, now they were on the screens, so everyone at the party could watch Chloe being a bitch when in reality she was just being real and keeping a true bitch at arm's length. I'll say this for Ana—she could sure fill a Jumbotron.

"Oh, pretty please?" Ana said, so shrill. Chloe relented and went with her old rival over to the event's exclusive photographer, a shrimp with thick glasses and poor personal hygiene who swore to God that this photo was a favor for *Us* and would never show up anywhere else.

"It's fine," Chloe said, aware that everyone must be talking about what good friends she was with Ana Cannon. Maybe Astrid would set them up for Season Two of *Magdalena Girl*. It would be easy enough to change the title to *Magdalena Girls*, right?

"So have you seen Joey?" Ana asked between her tightly-clenched teeth as the camera flashed away.

She had brass balls to bring up the guy they'd fought over. "No, why? Are you missing my foot in your face?" Chloe replied. Click, click, click. Part of rehab is saying you're sorry to people—but nowhere in the rules did it specify that Ana was a person.

"Oh, Chloe, that's ancient history. I just meant because he's here—I saw him and Lanny in the lobby. They're crashing." Click, click, click.

Chloe was shocked and stopped fake-smiling, so she could really smile. "Are you joking? They're here? Where?"

Ana pointed to the Jumbotron. "Not sure about Lanny, but I *think* that's Joey."

"Thanks, ladies," the photographer said. "I'll keep this one between us and *Us*."

Meanwhile, all of us were looking up at the closest of the big screens to see Joey locked in a passionate make-out session—with a guy.

"Clayton?" murmured the producer chick.

Joey, one of the biggest playas on the West Coast, was totally caught pressed into a corner making out with a hunky cameraman—oblivious to the fact that it was being televised to all the other party-goers. Soon, all the girls began a deafening "woo!" that got Joey's attention. He looked up to see himself and dropped Clayton like a dime-bag during a drug bust.

"This actually explains a lot," Chloe said, thinking to herself how happy she was that she was already over Joey. Because if she hadn't been, this might have driven her to crack.

"Yes," Ana replied. "Yes, it does."

Lanny was embracing Chloe before she realized he was there.

"Hey! Joey and I snuck in to surprise you. Are you surprised?" he asked, unaware of the commotion his fellow bedding crasher was causing.

Chloe just had to laugh. "Yes, Lanny. Pretty much."

Joey slinked out of sight, and Clayton grabbed his camera, heading back up to the VIP area to continue working. The Jumbotron found fresh victims—a washed-up soap actress passed out in a friend's lap and a high-powered publicist walking around with a serious expression and her right breast hanging out.

Joey's liplock wasn't the last of the evening's surprises.

It's not like we could have the kind of fun we were intended to have at the slumber party. We couldn't eat because we were trapped in the VIP area. We couldn't dance because there was no space in our fancy little prison. All we could do was look down at the crowd (in some cases, in every possible way) and people-watch, crack ourselves up, answer inane questions for the Magdalena cameras, and avoid Ana. Joey eventually found us and shrugged when we gave him faces that asked for an explanation.

"I don't know," he said. "I guess a lot of stuff became clear to me in rehab. Clayton was filming him as he said this, so he was guaranteed to look amazing once post-production was done.

"Poor . . . that Russian chick," Carrie said, caught halfway between compassion for Joey's soon-to-be ex and her limited memory.

Chloe's cell rang, and she almost screamed when she saw it was Ray. I sat next to her to listen in as much as possible since the music was blaring.

"Hey, Ray," Chloe said coyly. "I'm all dressed up for bed, and all I can think about is you. What's going on?"

Even from the half-assed way I was listening to her phone, I could tell this was not a call I should be eavesdropping on.

"I was gonna ask you the same thing, Chloe—*what is*

going on?" He didn't sound in love; he sounded enraged. "I can't believe you'd do this to me. How could you not even *tell* me?"

"Tell you what?" Chloe asked, her heart sinking. As she was talking, Astrid walked over to us with a magazine cover. It was a new issue of *Bitz*, and it had a picture of Chloe and *Chip*, of all people. It looked like it had been taken in front of the Sinbad, but that wasn't possible— Chloe had come directly in with Astrid when she found me earlier, and she hadn't left since. Plus, Chip wasn't within hundreds of miles. Yet it was definitely Chloe, and it was definitely Chip. Then it dawned on me—she was in that Missoni dress, the one she'd been wearing when she disappeared from Mode. She was also hugging and kissing Chip and holding a bouquet of flowers. The headline on the magazine was "CHLOE'S SECRET MARRIAGE." There was also an inset quote from Chip, stating, "I wouldn't be surprised if she was still on drugs."

Astrid was tapping the drugs quote with her bitten-off fingernail.

Chloe was speechless, but Ray wasn't. "Chloe, come on. Don't tell me you don't know what I'm talking about. It's on TV and all over the Internet. There's pictures— Chloe, you got married to Chip, and you didn't tell me. Did you think I'd never find out? I just can't believe this. I'll never get over it."

Then Ray hung up.

"Chloe, what's this about?" Peggy demanded.

"I . . . don't know," she said, looking to me. I sure didn't have any advice. I want elephants at my wedding, not pink elephants. But I knew right away that if Chloe really had gone off to Vegas and married Chip during that week she was missing, she had definitely been under the influence and didn't remember it—it's not that she was trying to hide it from anyone. And if that was true, it was just as true that Chip *was* hiding it. Until now, when it would gain him the maximum buck for his bang—it was no surprise that he was announcing his band was releasing a CD in the article.

"Where's that damn *Bitz* girl?" Chloe asked, looking around.

"Never mind her," Astrid said without a trace of empathy. "You're in a huge amount of trouble, Miss Parker. Not only are you causing bad press with your shenanigans, but I just got your urinalysis results back. You have tested positive."

Everyone on the entire VIP level shut up and stared at Astrid, then at Chloe. It was very U.S. Open.

"For . . . what?" Chloe managed to choke out.

"For just about *everything*," Astrid said. People gasped. Peggy didn't waste any time climbing right down Chloe's throat.

"Chloe, how could you do this to me?" she shouted. "How could you lie? How could you do this to yourself? Do you have zero respect for your body?" I'd never seen Peggy so choked with rage. But I'd also never seen Chloe so bewildered, even back in her cokehead days—I knew without having to ask that she had not fallen off the wagon. There had to be a mistake.

"Mom, no!" Chloe said, trying to remain calm. "No. I did *not* mess up. Astrid messed up. The results are wrong. They're just plain wrong."

"Chloe, don't. Don't lie to me. I didn't come to Las Vegas to get lied to. I came here to support you. And you've gone and made that a losing proposition. You've made a fool of us all, Chloe, all of us who love you." Peggy had stopped shouting, but her quiet voice had the same impact as most people's loud voices. "You've made a fool of yourself, too. Excuse me." With that, Peggy left.

The Magdalena cameras, thrilled to finally have the down to counter the up, the salt to chase the sweet, the agony to replace the ecstasy, did the only thing they knew how—they zoomed in on Chloe's expression of utter shock and sadness.

Pissed Off

ALL OF US have bad days. All of us make mistakes. And, if you're religious, all of us commit sins. We're flawed at the genetic level—it's what makes us human. But when you're famous, your flaws are magnified in the same way a jeweler's eyeglass reveals the white specks in a flawed diamond. When you're famous, your flaws are magnified and shown to everyone as a warning of how *not* to be and as an entertainment, instead of as what they really are—just proof that you're like everybody else.

But even though Chloe might have been able to handle the embarrassment of being Chip's unwitting wife, it was very difficult for her to deal with losing a promising relationship with Ray before it had fully begun, on top of losing her own mother's trust and respect, all on camera.

I was walking hand in hand with Chloe down the

longest hallway in the world, the one leading away from her humiliating slumber party and toward her penthouse suite at the cheesy Sinbad Resort & Casino.

As we walked, Chloe kept telling me things I already knew.

"I didn't use," she said firmly, going from stunned to angry. "I swear to you that I never used anything. No pills, no pot, no coke—no nothing."

"I believe you, Clo," I said. "You don't have to worry about me. Mik and Carrie and Lanny and Joey told you they believe you, too. You don't have to worry about us. We have to worry about figuring out a way to fix this up. We have to find out how this could happen, and we have to get you out of it."

"Yes," Chloe said with resolve. "You're right. I can't flip out and hide from this. I need to solve this."

As we approached her room, we turned and watched the camera crew disperse and head for their own rooms, conveniently arranged right outside Chloe's so there would be no late-night sneak-outs or any more privacy than was absolutely necessary.

Chloe's Barbara Eden Suite was sweet. It was gigantic—you couldn't rent a place that big in New York, and if you bought a place that size in L.A., we're talking multiple millions. But if it *had* been an L.A. pad and you bought it, the first thing you'd have to do is renovate. The Persian motif was haywire, with fake gold Arabic script and cat statues everywhere. The bed had what looked like reams of netting around it, straight out of somebody's warped vision of what a sheik's inner sanctum might look like. It was so Sinbad, it was good.

We walked in and immediately began changing into something less comfortable—that slumber wear was fun for the first hour but walking around in negligees got tired fast.

Clothed, we sat on the humongous, overstuffed couch, which was upholstered in a tasteful fabric that had miniature mosques all over it. It wasn't too surprising that the Sinbad had been sold and would be converted into a country-and-western themed complex.

"We need a strategy," I said. "First, what do you remember about marrying Chip? If anything?"

"I don't remember a minute of it," Chloe said. "I guess it happened here at the Sinbad from the pictures *Bitz* had. That's why it looks so familiar. But I don't remember marrying him. How scary is that?"

"Which part? Marrying Chip or forgetting about it?" We laughed, but our task at hand was serious.

"Well, you need to have your people contact Chip's people and demand proof of the wedding," I offered. "Then you need to demand an annulment."

"Oh, Nicole—they could annul the marriage, but how can I annul what Ray said to me? You heard him. He's furious. He must think I knew all along and was just playing him."

"Then you have to tell him you were in a bad place

then and truly didn't remember it. He'll believe you. He's just hurt. He's just being a *guy*, Chloe."

Chloe began to bawl out of nowhere and I let her. I started to cry a little bit, too. Everything was shit and we couldn't get our minds wrapped around a way to make things better.

"And I'm so going to get fired from Magdalena," Chloe said, stating the obvious. "There's no way that won't happen. Astrid was so pissed. Magdalena herself—you met her. She won't look the other way. I'll be the idiot who went from zero to hero and back to zero again in the space of a few months. I'll be a joke. I already am, probably."

"No—"

I tried to interrupt her, but she wouldn't let me.

"Nicole, don't try to tell me everything will be okay. It won't. If I don't have Ray in my life, there's no reason to believe I'll ever have another guy like him—I couldn't keep him, so why would I be able to keep anyone else? The show will be history. But the worst part of all is my mom hates me. I worked my whole life to live up to her expectations and when I finally did, I flunked the test. It's my mom! And she doesn't trust me. And she never will again."

I chewed on that. It was heavy and while Chloe had a flair for the melodramatic, in this case, she was just stating the facts. I felt terrible. I would have done anything to help her.

"I think I need to do a press conference or something and just apologize to everyone and beg everyone to forgive me and to believe me that I didn't have a relapse; I didn't let them down."

When a third voice echoed in the room, one that wasn't mine or Chloe's, we both jumped a mile. "That won't be necessary."

Chloe and I turned toward the bathroom, where a lone figure stood in a pair of cheap PJs and well-worn slippers. It was Liz Chan, the *Bitz* reporter. And she was standing in Chloe's room.

"You were hiding in the bathroom?" I yelled at her, ready to kick her ass back to L.A.

"How did you get in here?" Chloe demanded.

Liz was trembling all over, clutching a copy of her magazine and a microcassette recorder. Her face was twisted into a pathetic half-sob like an impressionable girl sitting in the audience of a tragic movie. And that's exactly what Chloe's speech had been like to her—something out of a movie.

Celebrity reporters are a strange bunch who usually fall into one of two camps: jealous haters or fans with columns. The haters spend all their time snarkily tearing celebrities apart, accentuating the negative in every story. They resent stars for having so much and would be the first to justify even the most invasive journalistic practices with a callous, "They're stars—it's part of the job." The fans are girls and gays who grew up making scrapbooks of their idols, majored in English, and moved to New York or L.A. in order to work for a glossy magazine and therefore have a valid excuse for following celebrities everywhere they go. Some of the fan variety can be as nuts as the haters—more—but most are sweet inside, full of genuine admiration for stars, and burning with a desire to get closer to them in any way possible.

Before Chloe could tear her limb from limb, Liz spoke, revealing herself to be the fan variety of reporter, and revealing something far more shocking, too: "I can't do this to you anymore, Chloe. You need to know the truth. You're not married. And you didn't flunk your pee test. It's all made up. And I can prove it."

She held the recorder out to us like a priest offering communion. We looked at each other, then we listened to the tape.

What we learned from the reporter and her recorder was that you never can tell who's got your back and who's got it just to have the opportunity to stab you in it.

Chloe's story has another villain besides drugs: Astrid Dillinger.

Liz sat between us and told us the whole sordid story: Astrid had been feeding *Bitz* bits and pieces of Chloe and Simone's lives from Day One. In exchange for personal pay-offs and enhanced coverage of Magdalena, Astrid had tipped off *Bitz* about the sudden reappearance of Freddy, she'd handed them the scoop about Simone's firing and she'd made a pact with Chip over the fake wedding story. And Liz had a lot of it on tape.

"I didn't marry Chip?" Chloe asked.

Liz shook her head. "No. You *did* come here to Las Vegas and gamble and stuff and go to a strip club, but everybody does that here."

"Strip club . . ." Chloe repeated. "Now *that* sounds more like Chip than marriage does."

The worst of it wasn't all the dimestore betrayals Astrid had perpetrated on a daily basis—those were all contemptible and enough to tick Chloe off, but they were things she would get over. The worst of it was the urine test.

"You didn't test positive," Liz said. "She faked the results. I mean, the results are real—it just wasn't your pee. Astrid paid for some druggy pee and switched it with yours. Then she alerted *Bitz*. That's how it works." She seemed relieved to be 'fessing up.

"But I don't get it," I said. "From what Chloe's tells me, Magdalena herself is very anti-drugs. And Astrid is enforcing that rule with the drug tests. What does Astrid get out of setting Chloe up?"

"Things changed when the commercials turned into a series," Liz said.

"That happened *last night*," Chloe interjected. "It hasn't even been officially announced."

"No," Liz said. "Astrid's been planning that for weeks. That's why I knew about it before you did. The show's producers need drama, so Astrid came up with this. That's why she invited your mother here—she knew after you tested positive, you'd have a huge fight and it would make for great TV. And she knew that when it got out that you'd flunked the test, it would be a huge scandal. The thing is, she also knew you would deny you tested positive and demand a re-test. Then you'd test clean and the Magdalena company would announce there was a mix-up. That way, more drama. And you triumph. And so does Magdalena. And the show."

"Why are you telling us this?" I asked, suspicious.

Liz looked downward and struggled to vocalize what had been on her mind. "Because this is *not* what I signed up for. I don't think there's anything wrong with telling the truth about stars—about you. Maybe it was insensitive to surprise you with your birth father, but it wasn't made up. But listening to you talk just now, I realized I couldn't let this go on. It's not real. It's made up. And it's caused you terrible pain. And I'm sorry. I'm really sorry, Chloe."

Chloe wasn't exactly going to hug her and put her on her buddy list, but she was grateful. There was no reason for Liz to be doing what she was doing other than that it was the right thing to do. And that was something Chloe would admire—and aspire to.

Her cell rang and she glanced down to see who it was, fully intending not to answer. Her eyes widened and she looked at me. "It's . . . Ray."

"Take it!" Liz and I said at once.

Chloe answered. "Hi," she said, in the same way I'd once greeted her after an awful fight we'd had.

"Chloe," Ray said to her, "I'm so glad I reached you. I heard the news about the, uh, drug test. I just wanted to tell you . . . I don't care about that Chip guy. I don't care if you're married or whatever. I want to be with you, and I want you to know that I'm here for you. If you're back on drugs, I want you to go back to rehab and I'll help you more this time. I—"

"Ray," Chloe said, stopping him. "You've already said everything you need to. I love you for saying all of that. I love you."

"Me, too," Ray said.

"Ray, I have to call you back because I have some business to attend to. But I need you to know that I never married Chip—it's a tabloid lie. And I never relapsed. That was also a rumor. But we'll talk more soon. I'll be back in L.A. by tomorrow."

"I don't understand—it's all not true? And tomorrow? Your schedule has you going to New York for events and stuff. I didn't expect you back here for a long time."

"I'll see you tomorrow. That's a promise."

CHAPTER

The "Bitz" Hits The Fan

C HLOE, DON'T COME see me right now," Peggy said sternly through her hotel door. "You don't want to see your mother right now—trust me."

Chloe wouldn't relent. Liz and I were standing behind her—in more ways than one.

"Mom, open this door right now. We *need* to talk. I *mean* it."

Eventually, the door cracked open and Chloe stepped inside. We didn't want to intrude, so we waited outside. I'd get the entire scoop later and, in a way, so would Liz.

Peggy had thrown blankets over her suite's windows in an effort to recreate her room at home in the Sinbad. It didn't work out too well, but the room *was* kind of dark. It didn't feel like a sanctuary so much as it felt like a never-used closet, though—she'd brought along countless designer outfits for the two day trip and had bought a few new ones in the hotel boutique, judging from the fresh boxes stacked along the wall.

"Chloe, I don't know what there is to say," Peggy stated flatly.

"There's plenty to say," Chloe said. "For one thing, the rumors about me marrying Chip? Fake. That reporter out there told me so and she has tapes implicating the Magdalena people in it. They were doing it for publicity and for my show to be controversial. The same goes for the drug test, Mom. I'm clean. Just like I told you."

Her mother listened, her face tipping nothing of what was going through her mind.

"What do you have to say to that?" Chloe prompted.

Peggy didn't have *anything* to say to that. She just collapsed onto her bed as if her spirit had left her body.

"Mom!" Chloe ran to her, fearing her mother had had a heart attack or worse.

But Peggy was not unconscious or having any kind of an attack. She was just relieved. She later told Chloe that in that moment, it felt like a thousand-pound weight had suddenly been lifted from her shoulders, one she'd never known she'd been carrying her whole life.

"Chloe," Peggy said with joy. "Chloe, you didn't . . . I'm so happy. I can't tell you."

After an initial spurt of relief that her mom was okay, Chloe went back to being resentful. "Mom, can't you even apologize for not believing me? You didn't even let me defend myself up there. You fell right into their trap. They knew they could count on you to lose your temper and yell at me. Don't you have anything to say about living *down* to people's expectations?"

Peggy smiled sadly and reached for her daughter's hand, clasping it tightly. Her own hand was adorned with three beautiful rings—the diamond wedding ring she'd never removed ("It's too pretty to get rid of—unlike your father"), a beautiful emerald set in platinum that had been her mother's, and a sparkly platinum band she'd bought herself when she turned 50 to cheer herself up.

"Chloe—I can't apologize for the way I acted. I know I was wrong to doubt you, but you should try to understand . . . I wasn't doubting *you* as much as I was doubting *myself*."

Beginning to cry, Chloe said, "Mom, I don't understand . . ."

"I know, baby," Peggy said softly. "I know you don't. I didn't either, not for a long time. It's . . . because I adopted you, because I took you away from that woman who wasn't good enough to be your mother—I chose you—I feel extra responsible for everything about you. I have to always be good enough, much better than her, or I'm . . . a fraud. When you do good, I'm so fulfilled I can hardly stand it. When you do bad, I'm not really mad at *you*, I'm ashamed of *myself* as a mother. You've always been my perfect ballerina girl—you know that? So if you make a mistake, the only explanation is that somewhere along the line, *I have failed you.*"

Chloe hugged her mom as if she'd never stop.

"Mommy, I love you. I do. Don't ever feel that way again. I want you to know that I'll make mistakes from time to time, but they'll never be because of you. I'm grown. I'm in control of my life now. I promise. Okay? Okay, Mom?"

Peggy was crying, too—a sight Chloe wasn't used to. With Peggy, it was usually anger more than sadness, yelling over crying. But it was a new day for both of them.

"Yes, Chloe, I promise you that I won't forget this talk."

After a few more minutes basking in each other's presence, Peggy wiped her nose with a tissue and asked, "Now what in the hell are we going to do about that terrible woman, that Astrid?"

CHAPTER  22

Hiatus

SOME TV SHOWS end when they're canceled after long, successful, record-breaking runs. Others end almost before they've begun, the victim of poor ratings thanks to lousy time slots, poor promotion, or unappealing stars. But the only TV show ever to be spun off of a commercial ended with a press release, albeit one written by a woman who was on her way out the door after a lifetime of perhaps too devoted service, and it ended before it had ever even hit the air.

When Chloe showed up at Astrid's door in the middle of the night, Liz at her side, Astrid denied everything to the hilt, begged for mercy and insisted it would all be fixed in future episodes and finally, fighting a losing battle, aged ten years and agreed that it would be best for her to have a midnight conference call with Magdalena to tell her the truth about everything. Chloe may have signed a contract for the series, but she had the company (or at least its agent) dead to rights, caught red-handed committing fraud.

Magdalena's voice on speaker phone was almost as daunting as Peggy's at her worst in person. Peggy nodded with respect as she listened to Magdalena dressing Astrid down and threatening everything from legal action to a contract on her life.

Finally, Magdalena said simply, "Astrid, you're a poor excuse for a daughter. And you're fired."

We couldn't believe it. "You mean, Astrid is your daughter?" Chloe asked.

"Yes," Magdalena said. "It's not a secret."

"But, I mean . . . you just never mentioned it before," Chloe said.

"If she were *your* daughter," Magdalena replied, "would *you* shout it from the rooftops?"

When we left Astrid, she was still putting the finishing touches on that press release, the one that would go to *Bitz* first and the rest of the planet immediately thereafter. In it, the true results of Chloe's drug test would be revealed, a corporate apology would be issued and Chloe's departure from the Magdalena commercial would be announced. "I'm thankful to Magdalena for the opportunity," Chloe's quote ran, "and I'm grateful that they would allow me my freedom from future commitments so I can spend some time with my family and friends and begin to focus on putting together my debut CD." Those rumors that Magdalena's commercials were about to become an MTV2 reality series? False. "While a series was discussed," Magdalena marketing executive Astrid Dillinger was quoted as saying, "it was ultimately decided that the latest Magdalena campaign had run its course. We wish Chloe all the very best of luck and sincerely apologize for the confusion that occurred in Las Vegas last evening."

The very next issue of *Bitz* was short on gossip and long on rehash since their reporter in the field, Liz Chan, had flown the coop. Liz was in the final phases of contract negotiations for a new position at the rival celebrity magazine *Wink*, the spiritual opposite of *Bitz* with its ultra-positive stories and star exclusives. The next cover of *Wink* was of Chloe Parker jumping into the Sinbad pool in her MTV Versace dress while all of her best friends bobbed in the waves around her. Inside, she gave page after page of juicy secrets about her Magdalena experience, including lots of stuff her confidentiality agreement would typically have forbidden—but she didn't expect Magdalena would sue her for it.

Or for anything else she ever decided to say—or to tell me so I could write about it for that matter.

CHAPTER 23

Liner Notes

I F WE WEREN'T A COUPLE BEFORE, we are now," DJ Ray said, nudging Chloe and pointing out the lurking paparazzi shooting them as they entered Mode.

"You can't stop the news," Chloe said, dazzling in a fresh new Chloé sent by Phoebe Philo herself. She smiled; she liked the idea of them as a couple as much as the tabloids did.

It was her first time returning to Mode since her meltdown when she'd kicked Ana Cannon in the face—which, granted, you didn't need to be on drugs to want to do real bad. At first, she shuddered when she walked in. But she got over it. Chloe had a lot to be happy about.

Six months after the last of her Magdalena commercials had ended, Chloe had finished recording a CD that would be released before the end of the year. She'd worked on it with Joey, whose compositions had helped inspire some of her best lyrics, and with Ray, who co-wrote songs and helped arrange the track that she felt in her bones would be the lead single.

Most important, her CD had been produced by Julius Parker. He'd finally forgiven Chloe her flaws.

Chloe was in every magazine thanks to Magdalena, and she'd been able to pull strings to have Mikela and Carrie be the next Magdalena friends. Chloe had warned them they'd be tested personally if they accepted the gig, but something told her Magdalena, minus Astrid, would not go *quite* so far off the deep end as they had with her and Simone.

Lanny was throwing Chloe a bash at Mode to celebrate all of this and of course the most important thing that had happened lately—her engagement to DJ Ray.

Ray had found a unique way to propose.

Waiting for the valet outside a restaurant, Chloe and Ray got kind of tired of being sitting ducks for the paps and decided to duck out and take a walk together down Robertson to that boring part of Wilshire.

It was a part of L.A. that Chloe had driven by a million times but never really looked at. Walking around with Ray, talking about rehab and music and just dumb stuff like *Austin Powers* or whatever, Chloe found herself noticing much more, like her body and mind were opening up and she was becoming more aware of everything.

As much as Chloe wanted to, they didn't hold hands,

but they did walk so close together that the backs of their hands kept touching—which bizarrely felt totally sexy. As much as she wanted to throw him to the pavement and kiss every inch of his body, just having the slight touch of the back of Ray's hand barely touching hers registered as an erotic highlight of her life.

Ray's ears were ruby-red all night long, which told her he had something on his mind—but she couldn't guess what.

They'd returned to the valet right before they closed and it wasn't until she melted into the leather of her silver Merc that she realized that all the walking they had done had given her blisters on both her feet.

As they said good-bye, instead of kissing, Ray asked her to reach into the breast pocket of the trendy corduroy jacket he had on over his usual ratty-but-chic T-shirt. Chloe had expected to find anything but what she found— a dazzling diamond engagement ring.

"Oh, my God . . ." Chloe whispered.

"Chloe," Ray said, his face now entirely ruby-colored just like his ears, "will you marry me?"

She tried to talk but she couldn't. When she imagined this moment in her head, she sort of thought her life would flash before her eyes—but it didn't. She looked into those beautiful eyes and all she saw was him and all she felt was love.

Then she looked down at that beautiful diamond. She didn't want to know how much Ray had paid for it because that had nothing to do with its real value. Its real value was that it meant Ray accepted and loved her, and that for all the flaws and foibles of her past, she was someone he wanted to build a future with. She just kept staring at it, smiling, unable to move.

"You better come in so we can show my mom because she's going to want to talk to you about taking good care of me," Chloe said. "And yes—I will!"

Now, back at Mode for an engagement bash, los fiancés made a splashy entry, drawing cheers from their supporters. I like to think that mine were the loudest.

Before she got too caught up with all her old friends, I had some business to take care of with Chloe.

"Remember this?" I asked her, dangling that amazing chandelier diamond earring in front of her, causing white lights and rainbows to dance across her cheeks.

"Oh, my God! I was beginning to think that thing was gone forever. I can't believe you kept it safe for me all this time, Nicole!"

"I'm just sorry it took me so long to return it to you."

Chloe gave me a totally fierce hug, like she really wanted me to feel it. When she broke it, she immediately took out one of the studs she was wearing and started putting on the chandelier.

"Look," she said holding her ring up next to her ear, her voice trembling with Christmas-morning joy. "It matches perfectly."

She was right, it did match—and perfectly. The tiny

diamonds in the earrings were like mini-versions of the emerald-cut rock that Ray had given her, like they were a bunch of little promises to go with the one big promise.

I wondered if she was thinking the same thing while she was checking herself out in the top-secret mirror in the green Balenciaga bag that had become one of her latest signature items. (For the record I got mine before she got hers. But what can I say? She wears the thing well.)

"I was going to give it back to you a while ago," I told her, "but I thought I should wait until things calmed down with you. Tonight seemed right."

She giggled and we both cracked up when she produced the other earring from her bag—we were so on the same wavelength it was scary. "I somehow knew you would have it for me tonight," she laughed, putting the second one in. "I'm glad you waited," she said, sliding out to hit the dance floor because Ray had just put on Missy Elliott, one of Chloe's all-time faves. "I appreciate them much more now. I mean as much as I loved these when Dad gave them to me, I love them even more now."

Carrie and Mikela met Chloe on the dance floor, while the boys—so typical—stayed in the booth and talked with Ray. Chloe was so happy to be with her friends and dancing to one of her favorite songs that her fiancé was playing. She kept shooting smiles and glances over at Ray, her eyes twinkling as brightly as both her newest and oldest favorite accessories, on her finger and in her ears.

I guess that's the thing about diamonds—they're the

most valuable things in the world, but what really makes them priceless is the people that give them to you. They may signify wealth, but they can actually mean so much more—like commitment, family, and love. And there's nothing like a perfect diamond to remind you that you'll never be perfect—the truth is, all you can do is try.

Acknowledgments

I would like to thank my mom and dad for all of their unconditional love and support. And to my Adam, thank you for being my best friend, my teacher, and my Prince!

I would also like to thank the following people whom I love and adore:

Mathu Anderson

The Azoff Family

Michael Broussard

Nancy Davis

Jonathon Erlich

Masha Gordon

Cindy Guagenti

William Hawkes

Honey, Foxy, Shalom, Muggsy

Annie Jagger

ACKNOWLEDGMENTS

Kidada Jones

Oliver Jones

Quincy Jones

Andy Lecompte

Jan Miller

Karen Moss

Judith Regan

Matthew Rettenmund

Larry Shire

Sofia and Miles

Robert Strent

Tara Sweeny

Rachel Zoe

Everyone at CAA

Everyone at ReganBooks and HarperCollins

Everyone at UTA